PILLAGE

PILLAGE

Miss Rosen Editions

© 2009 powerHouse Cultural Entertainment, Inc.
Text © 2009 Brantly Martin

Published in the United States by powerHouse Books,
a division of powerHouse Cultural Entertainment, Inc.
37 Main Street, Brooklyn, NY 11201-1021
telephone 212 604 9074, fax 212 366 5247
e-mail: pillage@powerHouseBooks.com
website: www.powerHouseBooks.com

First edition, 2009

Library of Congress Cataloging-in-Publication Data:

Martin, Brantly.
  Pillage / by Brantly Martin.
     p. cm.
  ISBN 978-1-57687-495-0 (hardcover)
  1. Upper class--New York (State)--New York--Fiction. 2. Manhattan (New York, N.Y.)--
Fiction. I. Title.
  PS3613.A77776P56 2009
  813'.6--dc22
                          2008043569

Hardcover ISBN 978-1-57687-495-0

Printing and binding by Everbest Printing Company through Four Colour Imports

Cover art direction by Valentina Ilardi
Cover photo and author photo by Billy & Hells
Book design by Robert Avellan

A complete catalog of powerHouse Books and Limited Editions is available upon request;
please call, write, or visit our website.

10 9 8 7 6 5 4 3 2 1

Printed and bound in China

PILLAGE

by
Brantly Martin

pH powerHouse Books Brooklyn, NY

"The autobiographical novel, which Emerson predicted would grow in importance with time, has replaced the great confessions. It is not a mixture of truth and fiction, this genre of literature, but an expansion and deepening of truth. It is more authentic, more veridical, than the diary. It is not the flimsy truth of facts, which the authors of these autobiographical novels offer but the truth of emotion, reflection and understanding, truth digested and assimilated. The being revealing himself does so on all levels simultaneously."

—Henry Miller

"It isn't up to the painter to define the symbols. Otherwise it would be better if he wrote them out in so many words! The public who look at the picture must interpret the symbols as they understand them."

—Pablo Picasso

everything's addicting, even the truth

One

Hanging out at The Sheik's you could learn everything you need to know about The Island. About Amoeba. He lives at 666 Madison, 13th floor.

To be truthful, I don't hang out there. I hide out. I come to after a blackout. I rationalize and seek a co-signer.

The Sheik's apartment is a 24-hour onslaught. Thousands of images on rotation, spread over six 30-inch monitors. Ten seconds of manufactured perfection. One after another.

I'm the only one that's allowed in.

He used to not let me see the befores, that was a long time ago. Now? I've seen them all. Every cover for *Belle*, *Stogue*, *Gismo*. Every contrived Amoeban Popesse that forgot to shave her cunt before the photo shoot. Every lard-infested, lip-synching, beauty pageant daughter driving the Amoeban youth to Troll-Mart. Every dignified same undone.

Sheik, we need more cleavage here, this is for French Belle...
Sheik, we need you to take 50 pounds off this same, slim the hips, perk the tits...
Add some nipple...
Sheik, the cat is too fat...yes, the cat...

The Sheik smokes 15 joints a day. The man is never without a joint in his hand. Never. He does yip once a year and tries to stab people, plants.

He is the only person in the Galaxy I trust implicitly with the content of my dreams.

For twelve years The Sheik has put the final touches on every image that's caused a Midwestern same's throat to feel her finger. He's the only pure artist I know. Artist for hire.

photoshop

Photoshop on enriched uranium. Ayatollah. The Sheik could make me pinned on yip, saucered on D. Aeronymous trim. Give Fireman back his chest hair. Make Noddy trackless.

The Island's microcosm and future. A creator of Amoeban fantasies. The reason you masturbate and buy diet pills.

He is both proactive and reactionary. Court jester and playwright.

He doesn't mind if I slam speedballs in his crib.

A native Islander, The Sheik rarely leaves his apartment before midnight. I once tempted him into accompanying me to Amsterdam, he made it all the way to the Midtown Tunnel before having a panic attack and leaping from the car.

The Island's projection of the Amoeban dream is played out every day at 666 Madison. It's where the cattle get branded. Ten hours on the eyes. Three days on the tits, nipples. Teeth. Lips. Forehead. Inner thighs. Hair. Years.

scars

Lo que sea. It's a great place to drink beer and rip some lines.

use once and destroy
use u-100 insulin only

Houston   Austin   El Paso   Mexico City   Chicago   New
Orleans   Boston   Denver   Miami   London   Paris   Milan
Rome   Amsterdam   Tenochtitlan   Brussels   Berlin   Hamburg
Munich   Prague   Moscow   St. Pete   Stockholm   Uptown
Athens   Halkidiki   Thessaloniki   Rotterdam   Antwerp
Bangkok   Authaya   Chiang Mai   Luangprbong   Gleisica   Ho
Chi Minh   Phnom Penh   Babylon   Hanoi   Sapa   Delhi   Siem
Reap   Shianoukville   Jakarta   Scrotum   Bali   Montreal
Vancouver   Calgary   Medicine Hat   Winnipeg   Havana
Matamoros   Fetus   Cadequés   Anal Shank   Caracas   Santiago
Rio   São Paulo   San Salvador   Buenos Aires   Punta
Montevideo   Seattle Darby A   Saba   Jacksonville   Empty
Baggies   Philadelphia   Woodstock   Wernersville   St. Charles
Limbic   St. Louis   Dallas   Tokyo   Lisbon   Perpignan
Barcelona   Dropper's Neck   Bangladesh   Stems   Lost Aimless
The Island.

the coke   yack   gack   crack   gear   smack   ya ba   poppers
acid   speed   ecstasy   meth   g   k   peyote   luudes   d   opium
morphine vicodin mdma   dust   shrooms   hash   pure   powder
shooting   smoking   snorting   whiskey   tequila   bourbon
vodka   gin   reds   whites   beer   cigs   stoges   fags   spirits   resin

Oh dear lord all of it. Sum it up, throw it in my ass—a
suppository. Allow me to regurgitate it for you.

Two

I contemplate my place.

Not 109 Spring, my place in the world. The Galaxy, Milky Way and beyond. The Drake's Equation. The possibilities, the lack of. 27 years.

Sweating like a priest in the Reeperbahn, I stroll my loft. Blue eyes black, the two love valleys sunk deep into my sarong's drought. Posing and flowing, introspecting and projecting. No one is there. Everyone's there! Alone, surrounded, ridiculous, beautiful, superfluous, divine, virile, impotent. Ahh...crack.

My orbit is cocaine—my sun, my god. I'll be born again tomorrow, or that tomorrow. But tonight the axis is set. My satellites are in motion, perpetual.

One can get mad at his satellites, but to denounce them would be to give up one's star status.

Dark, Lark, and the same sames carry on their pre-determined fates in the living room—no evolution, just revolution. Corona, cocaine, Patrón, stems, rocks. One of the sames sweats a particular blend of whorish exuberance. A sommelier might describe it to the table as a Red-Light district, Patpong road, Upper East Side, South of France, Rio Grande Valley fusion— table wine.

I settle opposite my only window—ribs protruding, rest of the bone family available. Blue and white oval flags flapping red and black, I'm seeing life through an alternate lens. My speech pattern matched only by heartbeats per minute.

'I don't know…I don't really like a guy all metro,' declares Dulce, hitting shuffle on the iPod.

'I know honey, but do you really wanna feel back hair on some fella? I know I don't, especially if he's rich and I gotta stick it out for a bit.' Thanks Brittice.

'Oh my gaawd, I know,' fumbles coke-lipped same same number three, jolting me into speaking condition.

'Well my dear, you can't feed from both tits. We live in The Island, the goddamn Eden of loot, the fucking cock of capitalism! We're fisted daily with the rules of engagement, gotta take the good with the bad, yin-yang, all that shit. The exact epidemic that allows all these ladder dwellers to be rewarded for getting electrolysis, teeth-whitening, manicures, pedicures, Portofino memberships, bi-weekly haircuts…all the while taking out just enough time to name drop at the latest jappy run restaurant that paid its way into *Page Fix*…one by one proliferating anti-thought and diseasing the world with it…well that's why we have the iPod and cocaine home delivery.'

Soapbox clearly undermined by the yip, I journey to genuflect in the mirror. Rock-filled stem in hand, I move to firing position.

zippo? fire
stem? lit
suck. hard
exhale

I begin to roam again, thankful I've expounded some thoughts prior to departure.

Dulce remains detached in conversation: *where are you from…yeah…I love Paris…oh my god, I slept with him too…I know for such a big guy…can you pass the bag…yeah…*

'So girls, have you ever had a hit blown up your arse?'

Dark Hose has a way with words. His cousin Lark Taker looks on in astonishment. As unlikely as it might seem, the hit up your ass line invariably returns the intended results. No sooner has Dark inhaled the rock than Brittice pulls down her panties and is on all fours.

Maxing out all lung capacity, Dark takes off his sarong, crawls over to the same—balls pendulating—and unleashes a funnel cloud of rock, up her ass. A couple uninvited licks follow.

'Oh wow, that was...uhmm...I'm fucked up.'

'It's a bloody rush my love.'

Dulce knows the rush well. She is a creature without guilt—no rear view, no binoculars. She knows I live with my same, but Slutskia's in Taiwan. Until she comes back there's nothing to think about, other than yack. *Vida es simple.*

The shenanigans carry on between Dark and the sames, a regular neighborhood upperware party.

Living in the moment has its moments—elapsing as they are. At this point in the game I enjoy ever shrinking bubbles of serenity.

past and future...(silence)...helicopters

Slutskia's good for half the rent, half the deposit, half the broker's fee, a tenth the time. It's possible I'm falling in love with Dulce. After all, Slutskia's been away for two months (we speak once a week and confess our love). At least that's what I reckon is coming through a three-second delay in Ruskenglish.

So yeah, I think I'm falling in love with Dulce—if I was mad enough to believe in such things.

I love you? currency, the biggest. Fuck the Dollar, Pound, Crown, Euro. And why not? You never need a deposit, guarantor, co-signer or credit approval. But make no mistake, it's always a loan with interest. And when the spurned come to collect...oh boy! I'd be ecstatic with two broken legs.

Dark has moved to my sauna—stems, rocks, and sames in tow.

My place. I'm on the third floor, straight shot with the stairs. You immediately take in the carpet—grey, very. Perhaps at one time it was lovely Korean black, not now. The first bathroom to the left is an all '70s tile-laden concoction, the stock of which nuevo rich Islanders scoff and trust fund Islanders marvel. Snorkeling forward in the cesspool of grey you bump into a Billy's Antique dining room table, the only window, an island on your right. The island floats on pseudo tile whose delta presents you with a washer/dryer, 50 cabinets, and 371 bottles of flavored whiskey from a past business deal gone awry.

Wading vomit stains, you take three steps down to the dying room. Lurking on the wall is the only thing of value in the place, conveniently the only thing that's not mine. Aside from the painting, there's two couches, a Sixth Avenue flea market iron rocking chair, turntables, loads of DVDs and books.

Up the stairs is an open bedroom, my quarters. A Slutskia bought flat-screen hangs on the wall, along with a picture of my dead *Abuela*, empty baggies, rigs, tinfoil, stoge boxes. Beneath the bed is a walk-in closet, sharing a wall with the sauna and the second bathroom. A hop away is the other bedroom.

With Dark in the sauna discussing the devil knows what, I'm eye-fucking Dulce. She's the only same I've come across where

yip dick is not an option. Not a once has her triple-pierced
shaved twat falsetto failed to bring me to attention.

Dulce. Indian-style on my white couch. Eskimo skin, red g-
string, portrait perfect flapper bangs—slave black. If she were
West African she'd be famished, in The Island she's just heavily
ribbed. The hip bone handles leading to her cunt were sculpted
by Jesus and Satan during a campaign stop in purgatory. Dulce's
smile could make serfs noble, pedophiles blush, Jews call their
father, Dalí rethink Gala. Arouse a eunuch. And her tits! A
famished villager with C's! At the right angle they even cover
her ribs. *And the nerve to want to get loaded after a session.* I
take back that I love you garbage. Dulce, the only same same in
the land that owns it—all of it. I met her inkless, she's now
Island Adorned three times over. I love her.

We devour rails, down Patrón.

Ascend to my quarters.

Copulate. Fornicate.

Another hit and I'm dog-paddling in thought.

the what ifs
Yack with no snipers, dope with no itch, beer with no calories,
blue eyes on crack, Fireman with no same addiction, Noddy with
no slamming, Aeronymous with discipline, Lousifer with
perspective, Slave straight, Tambourine on literature. Dulce as
Slutskia. Slutskia as Dulce. *Sanity?*

Despite my session with Dulce, I can't sleep. I bid her farewell
and get back to jaw grinding. *Is there any H here?* Xanax at
least? Dark, Lark, and crew gone, I plop down *sans* clothes on

my holy couch. Precisely how geeked I am beginning to reveal itself. I put on my iPod, hit shuffle.

♫*Just because you're paranoid don't mean they're not after you*♫

g thanks kurt

KNOCK KNOCK.   KNOCK KNOCK.   KNOCK KNOCK.

fuck

KNOCK KNOCK.   KNOCK KNOCK.   KNOCK KNOCK.

fight it Cracula, no one's there

KNOCK KNOCK.

Well maybe the neighbors heard the racket. There were three yacked up sames here, Dark and Lark. Maybe those bastards did something and bailed. Maybe they just want tea? After all I haven't broken bread with my neighbors in the year I've been here. That makes sense.

KNOCK KNOCK.

damn it, it's some dealer I've been avoiding

KNOCK KNOCK

fuck it

I dump out the rest of the gear on the table and roll a single. Right nostril, left nostril, right, left, right, left...I'm marching, a goddamn soldier in the army of yip. I don a sarong, grab my knife, and float to the door—the peephole. No one. *The fucker is hiding in the hall. Well I'm not waiting for him to shoot the*

door in. I open the door, blade in hand, step into the hall.
Nobody. Wait, coming up the stairs. *Son it's on.* I stealth to the
stairs, *I'll beat him to the punch.* As I glide, he ascends. Fate
intercedes and we are two feet away, separated by the landing.
My sarong falls to the floor. *No worries, I'll stab this
motherfucker naked.*

'Ahhh....Help!'

Mother of God, it's my upstairs neighbor. She's been in the
building since 1972 (only pays $500 a month). I'm naked,
sweating, and brandishing a switchblade. My candy-red cock at
half-mast.

'Ma'am, I'm sorry. I'm your neighbor.'

Retreat.

With sleep not an option, the helicopters, snipers, and anti-tank
missiles begin closing in. I decide to brave the world.

I slide on my black Levis, thermal, Hugo shearling, St. Mark's
scarf, Island Adorned hoodie, pupil-hiding shades and hit Spring.
The ghosts of Soho past all around—cheap lofts, graffiti, golden
eggs. Only now it's all been airbrushed, photoshopped to death.
The lofts no longer belong to artists, but to formulaic Amoebans
or Native gazillionaires. The only graffiti left, just down Spring,
is on death row since an inventor bought the building. The
phonies that are left all channeling the same slice of 80s. And
the same sames? Forget it, they think it's still happening. Please
don't get me started on the weekend—it's a fucking EU field
trip. I would have thought it impossible to extract every
Parmigiani-Exchange wearing, Smart Car-driving bastard and
deposit them on Dead Broadway. *Lo que sea.*

Escaping the Feds, CIA, KGB—I head east toward Mercer—passing what was Mekong and what is now Wrong Hunch. Could it be more tragic?

My paranoia subsided to a non-life threatening level I might be able to pull off a coffee at Balthazar.

Forging ahead, I feel the presence of something…something debilitatingly immense. He's catty-corner to me, heading west on the south side of Spring.

Aeronymous has a patented stroll—more like a meticulous waddle. He is a contorter, Cult member, friend. Moving forward he swallows the sidewalk like it's black spaghetti at Frank's. In spite of it being 15 degrees out, he has an iced coffee (extra sugar) in his left hand, a buy-one/get-one-pack-free Turkish gold stoge in his right. I'm not sure if I want to be seen or not.

Too late.

'Yo Cracula! What's up son?'

A quite familiar, and bastardly, superiority washes over me as I await his ever so difficult crossing of Spring.

Really studying the waddle for the first time, I can't ascertain how Aeronymous moves forward. To the naked, or cracked out eye, it appears as if he simply strides left and right. Perhaps he does, with his gargantuan girth pulling him forward. Throw in the alarming green BAPE sweater and you have an optical illusion—an endangered species—a waddling, Sidekick-wielding, chain-smoking urban wildebeest.

As he crosses Spring cabbies slam on their breaks, Range Rovers thank god for airbags, hot-dog vendors smile in anticipation.

'What's up Aeronymous?'

'Chillin son. What's the deal? How you been, I miss you son.'

Aeronymous never fails to greet as though you're a long-lost lover exiting customs at JFK.

'No different than I was two day ago son.'

'Word, I just saw Dulce going to Narc. Did you handle that son?'

Despite (because of?) the amount of space Aeronymous possesses in the world, I love him. So I'm never sure if sharing my exploits produces a vicarious kick or contributes to his medicating via parmesan.

'What the fuck do you think?'

'Word son, that bitch looked like she just got slayed.' A true wordsmith. 'I got some ass last night too son.'

Whenever Aeronymous is about to lie, his voice slips, his dome contorts, and his belly retracts.

'Yeah?'

Best of all his words go from an acceptable Native Downtown flow to Down Syndrome.

'Y e a h , y o u   k n o w   t h a t   g i r l
L a a n d i s? I   f u c k e d   h e r.'

Pandora has nothing on Aeronymous. Bordering the Chelsea green BAPE sweater to the south is a factory's worth of dark blue denim that hangs below his ass. North of BAPE is his breakfast — caked over both cheeks, bottom lip, and the gaps in his grill.

'Yeah son, I guess the bitches were hungry last night…hungry for pound cake son.'

The joke is outdated, not funny, and one of his staples. Nevertheless, it sends Aeronymous into a belly laugh for the ages, causing a seismic reaction in his mid-region.

Thrusting his head back—giggling and snorting—a tidal wave gives birth in his lower gut, sending a tsunami towards his breasts. 7A bacon and cheddar launch from his mouth, iced coffee and stoge goners. When the tsunami reaches his throat gravity takes over, sending it back to the earth, doubling him over—size 56 skid-marked white hanes revealed.

Time for a croissant.

Eastbound on Spring we trek. Approaching Broadway we are in front of Sari, a favorite hangout of contorters rapping to sames. Sitting outside is none other than the two Israeli brothers I've been looking for.

'Hey Aeronymous, where's the party tonight?'

'At Lame Lame son, you know I'm always holdin it down there.'

'Cool. See you tonight.'

'Do you know Cracula?'

Sure they do.

'Hi.' Hey.

'Don't shake my hand motherfucker.' Guess I'm still geeked. 'You know me, I live right down the street with my same, Slutskia.' Their *who me* game face on. 'Tall blonde Russian, big tits.' Skeed. 'Don't act stupid motherfuckers, I swear to god if either one of you says another word to her....' Geeked. Yipped. Whacked. Aeronymous and I cross Broadway.

'Yo son, what's up with that?'

'Nothing bro. Those idiots always have something smart to say to Slutskia, fuck that.'

'Word. You doing alright son? You slept?'

'Nah man.'

'I know now's not the time, but there is a better way Cracula. You need to join The Cult, stop doin all that shit.'

'Aeronymous I love you, but not now.'

'I feel you. When does Slutskia get back?'

'Tonight.'

'You peacing Dulce out?'

'Don't know if I can.'

'Word.'

Palabra.

'Yo son, you heard about Lousifer?'

Aeronymous, my own satellite radio. A 24-hour downtown Island newscast. Free of charge, but with health warnings.

Exposure in high doses to Aeronymous may cause the following symptoms. If they persist, run.

1. The relinquishing and subsequent broadcasting of your most personal moments/experiences.

2. An unwilling hypnotic state, leading one to wander aimlessly through Soho and/or the East Village in search of iced coffee, stoges, sames.

3. A steady rise in the use of **one** or **all** of the following words: son, mad, nigga, word, yo, peace.

4. A rising intake of coconut flan.

5. Random, high-pitched, and uncontrollable laughter.

'No Aeronymous, what's up with Lousifer?'

'Yo son, I was at Lame Lame last night with mad sames, and that nigga rolled in all cracked out...covered in fuckin blood son. I was like, yo you alright dude? He's like: *yeah, I just ran into some nigga that robbed me, fucked him up, what's good.* haa haaa... I was like, yo son, you're covered in fuckin blood...and he's like: *oh shit son, be back in thirty...* Then he just peaced...haaa haaaa.'

'Word?'

'Word, smashed some nigga's face in.'

I see.

'And yo, Fireman called me lookin for you.'

Yeah?

'He was getting a pedicure with some Brazilo same...says she's in love with him, but so are all her friends...haa haa. Doesn't know who to bring to dinner tonight. Says he has too many sames...haa haa. You comin tonight son? Ten o'clock at Lame Lame. I got mad sames comin son. Doing a birthday party for the same from the Hucci campaign.'

Yeah?

'Fuck yeah son. I got fitty sames comin after dinner son, gonna kill it son. Mad sames.' Sure.

'You speak to Noddy?'

'Son, that nigga was with me at Lame Lame last night too...all doped up. And I swear to God, he nods off right in the middle of talkin to some same, lights Leachal's hair on fire, falls face first in the ice...and pops up...like *yo it's all good son*...haaa haaa.'

Satellite radio, channel blast.

(crackberry text)
cracula I was talking about u 2day during my weekly 3 way thpiritual intervention and channeling session

both dim and my thpiritual adviser think it's time 4 u to accept a thpiritual path. i'm always hear 4 u! let me no if u need me to show u the lite

thpiritually yours, tambourine

'Son, who the fuck was that?'

'My X.'

'Word?'

'Inviting me to some sort of spiritual *ménage à trois* with her boyfriend.'

'haa haa.'

Ahh…Tambourine. My own Eta Carinae. Not so many moons ago she was spontaneous, sensual. Endless. She had capacity.

Now? Thpiritual. A goddamn wine sipper. Only dates satellites. Has it ALL figured out. *Lo que sea.*

Aeronymous and I reach our outpost.

'Yo son, coffee?'

'Black.'

We man our post, the bench splitting Balthazar pastry shop and restaurant.

'Yo, what's the deal kids?' It's Turbo.

'What up T?'

'Yo Turbo, how you been? Haven't seen you for a minute son.' Aeronymous and his customs greeting. He and Turbo are quickly lost in some asinine conversation that no doubt had a previous running.

'…word son, that's what I'm sayin. I'm from here son, I was born in The Island son…'

'Me too son, fuck that shit.'

In the United States of Amoeba, Amoebans have always been ready to judge who is an Amoeban and who isn't. First generation have always been looked at as outsiders, immigrants, scum. Islanders, being the brains of Amoeba, take this even further. To them I will always be an immigrant. Not just an immigrant, a Mexican. Spic. Wetback. If the Natives had their way, the GW, Williamsburg, and Brooklyn would be drawbridges. The Lincoln and Midtown blown up. They are forced to accept the notion of coexistence, but are always quick on the trigger of subtle reminding. *I grew up here son* or *back in the day*. Yeah, and forever shall you stay here. Son. Your island, your prison. Without your tired-ass references what the hell have you got? Alcatraz east. And when a Native dare leave The Island don't think they go five goddamn minutes without letting all comers know their derivation. If it isn't *back in the day* it's some uptown Native dropping private school names. To them I am forever a Mexican. *fucking bring it* Give me your menial jobs, your condescension, your nose up as I learn the native tongue. For I will turn it around and fuck the Native out of your daughters. Spread my Mexican seed and colonize you bastards. I will keep my back wet, the proudest Mexican alive. *Viva Mexico!* Fuck your border patrol, I'll swim up the Rio Grande to the Hudson. *Comprende?* And for my efforts you shall have Cracula offspring.

'Aeronymous, Turbo, I'm out. Gotta crash.'

'Word son.' Peace.

pounds

'Yo Crac, call The Fireman. He just sent me another text lookin for you.'

I'm sure The Fireman's day is going as did his life—planned, thought out, via systems. The man is a conductor. A manager of same sames, businesses, moments. No doubt he's juggling conference calls with banks, various partners around the globe, same same appointments. He is, after all, a same addict. What Noddy does for dope, Aeronymous does for slices, Lousifer does for flipping, I do for yip—he does for sames.

The man will start high, though never afraid of the bottom rung. Super sames to busted hyenas. Strangers to best friend's sames, no matter. Despite his mosh-pit of connections, his *good friends,* I'm his go-to guy for confiding, co-signing, boasting, and projecting. My indifference of late seems to have escaped him, taking my passive *I knows* and *sures* as an endorsement. These days I answer my phone less and less, though more a function of my lack of coherent daylight hours than a statement on The Fireman.

I'm light years away from able to get a credit card, a phone in my name, or request a credit report without breaking the system. Yet I remain the guarantor for all my friends' actions. *Sure Fireman, 15 is old enough...no doubt Aeronymous, another Demarco's pizza won't hurt...don't worry Noddy you're only 24, there's plenty of time to be an ex-addict...*Of course my co-signing ability is never stronger than with myself. *Slutskia won't find out...there's no way she has the hep...what's sharing a needle a couple times...I've nothing to do tomorrow, let's get 10 grams, five hookers and fucking do this...*The nation of rationalization.

I walk up my stairs, praying for no neighbor.

(crackberry ring)

'Yo man.'

'Wow Cracula, you actually answered.'

'Still up.'

'That's not surprising. You OK?'

The Fireman, for all his tragic faults, would die for me. Take a bullet. If only it didn't interfere with being able to extract pleasure, self-actualization, or Island fame through a same. And the man is brilliant, the top math professor in all of Amoeba. *El Jefe*. Can size up the common denominator stored deep inside any human being. *House music? Me too. Hip-Hop? Rock? Patrón? Beer? Sober? Gack head? Amoeban? Orthodox? Wiccan? Native? Eastern bloc? Me too.* The man could find the square root of pi if a same was at the end.

'I'm always good.'

'What's up for tonight, you gonna make it?'

Sure, why not.

'Your boy Aeronymous says he has twenty sames coming to dinner.'

'So...eight.'

'Five.' *palabra* 'Did I tell you about the new Brazilian that wants me?'

I'm sure you will.

'So I'm out with my good friends last night and this Brazilian same won't take her eyes off me. Then again, who can? I couldn't really talk to her though, I was with too many other sames. They all wanted me, I just look too damn good these days. It's hard sometimes.'

Yep.

'So, see you there? Ten o'clock at Lame Lame? Oh by the way, when does Slutskia get back?'

'Tomorrow night.'

'What're you gonna do about Dulce?'

'Couldn't tell ya.'

'OK, so I'll see you tonight. Ten o'clock.'

Always going out in control, The Fireman. I grab a bottle of whiskey, crawl into bed.

As much as coming down off coke sucks, it's the only time I feel alive.

estaba soñando

I strolled up Fifth Avenue into the opaque Island winter, unaware.
Comfort abounded.

I was alone, marching.
There was no time, no light, an eclipse.

Washington to Union Square an eternity,
I was the only living boy in The Island.

I skated, protested, freestyled.
sat on the steps and smoked

there was no life.

No black Israelites calling me devil, no sames,
no goth kids from the burbs.
No music.

i stood up, fell down, began to rise

Wings erupted from my shoulders, my fangs retracted.
I flapped and floated, alone in The Island.

subdued

For the first time neither vampire nor blood bank.

I faced north and spread my wings.
With one thrust I was floating above St. Patricks.

I smelled creatures below,
the only life in The Island.
I swooped down, wings spread,

walked to the gates.

i pulled and pulled—angels not welcome

Enraged, my wings fell to the steps.
Fangs returned, the gates flew open.

I walked step-less down the aisle, past the pews.
black suit adorned

There was a proceeding taking place, I was expected.

Approaching the altar it came to be that St. Patrick's had become
a courthouse of sorts, a cathedral nonetheless.

Above the altar were three crucifixions. To the left, Dulce was
willingly nailed to the cross—naked and motionless. A king
cobra was her tongue, unable to escape. flailing. spitting
venom. Her green eyes a black and red checkerboard.

To the right, Slutskia was freshly crucified. Still breathing,
bleeding. her eyes gone blank. She stared at me without
pleading, expecting me to provide salvation. Her tongue a
python, slowly wrapping itself around her neck. ready to kill the
pain

Directly above was Tambourine. Her blood scarcely alive. She
cried in waves of agony—Biblical screams. Pleading for me to
save her, to be human. Her eyes escaped life, my fangs grew.

Drowning out the death, Feather blindly floated above the
crucified. carelessly meandering the rafters, unaware of the
impending proceedings.

Below the soon-to-be deceased sat the panel of judges. To the
left sat my mother, certain to go against me. To the right sat my

brother, certain to go for me. In the middle was my father—but Abraham Lincoln—yet my father. The swing vote, the only judge I need convince.

The trial was to be humanity versus god. I took my seat on the right.

To my left sat god. Through an unfortunate series of events, god had become a deaf mute many years ago and was unable to represent himself. Speaking on his behalf would be George W. Lush. He sported baggy jeans, Dunks, a Rocawear hoodie, and platinum chain.

My father, Honest Abe, spoke. 'Mr. President, you are here to speak in defense of god, the almighty. Do you accept this responsibility?'

'No doubt son, let's do this nigga.'

'Cracula, you have been summoned here today to represent Amoeba and all of humanity. Do you accept this responsibility?'

I suppose.

'Mr. President, you may proceed with the opening arguments in defense of god.'

'Word. Well ya honor, let me start by sayin god is great. It's right to give him thanks and praise, ya feel me? If it weren't for god wouldn't none of us even be up in this motherfucker. I mean check it out, dude gave up his only son for us, for our sins and shit, and we all be sinners homey. Every damn thing I do be in the name of god. god loves Amoeba, we be the hand of god, and I be runnin this motherfucker accordingly. If it weren't for god...shit son, I might still be drinking the devil's juice, but he done saved my ass. This dude god, he wants freedom, he wants democracy, he wants the Amoeban way.'

Father Lincoln interjected. 'This freedom of which you speak, is it to be shared by all?'

'Yeah, more or less. I mean I ain't down with no fags, Muslims, artists, or no shit like that…but yeah homey, freedom.'

'Well sir…'

'Excuse me son, I mean ya honor. Just let me wrap this shit up real quick. I wanna close by sayin that I'm even down for most black dudes to have freedom, other than that New Orleans thing. Cause god loves those cats too, ya feel me? As far as humanity be, fuck that homey. You gotta love god, worship that nigga while you on earth. Only then you gonna be saved. I know so, he done told me. And I'm a man of conviction, that's my word son.'

'But hasn't god become a deaf mute, Mr. President?'

'You know what the fuck I mean.'

At this point I escaped my body and elevated above the proceedings, above the three dead bodies on crosses. Resting next to the oblivious Feather. *Or was she impervious?* The proceedings continued. My dream relegating me to the third.

'Cracula, you may now present the opening argument in defense of humanity.'

I grabbed a rafter, hoping I didn't fuck it up below.

'Thank you, your honor. First, I want to thank God for joining us today. It's a shame he's become a deaf-mute and unable to speak for himself.'

'Objection your honor! I was made the spokesperson for god fair and square.'

'Cracula, lest I remind you, we are not here to question the authority of the president to speak for god.'

g thanks dad

'In that case, allow me to speak on two points of the president's statement. First, the bastardizing of conviction. This ought be an outlawed word, your honor. There is no necessity for truth in conviction. The president continuously resorts to his *convictions*, and the *convictions* of the Amoeban people. A conviction is nothing more than a tightly gripped lie, an error so blatant it must evolve into a *conviction*. A conviction is unwavering and resistant to truth. A conviction is not retractable. A conviction is inhuman, your honor.'

'Objection homey! How dare he question my convictions in god. Yo son, by doin that he be questionin the convictions *of* god.'

'Overruled.'

Thanks Abe.

'Next is worship your honor. Does not worship of man, symbol, or deity drain one's soul? I'm sure if god weren't a deaf-mute…'

'Goddamn it ya honor, can you tell this nigga that we already done established that I'll be doin the speakin for God.'

'Sustained.'

What the hell am I doing down there?

'Your honor, would it not be downright sadistic for a father to want his son to worship him?'

"Are you questionin my love for my daddy Cracula? You motherfucker! Listen here you punk, I love my daddy. My daddy's the baddest motherfucker that ever done lived. Shit son, I started a war for my daddy. Don't make me send you to Iraq motherfucker!'

'Mr. President, are you still hitting the pipe?'

'That's it, you gonna die son...'

'Order, order.'

Three

(crackberry ring)
'Yeah…yes Aeronymous I'm coming. Ten o'clock, Lame
Lame. Yeah. Bye.'

No idea if I've slept or not. My eyes were closed, but my veins
are still transporting yip. Dumping it in my brain.

Half an hour later I muster the courage to sit up. My room is
unrecognizable, a landfill. A toxic zone where creatures subsist
on flavored whiskey, beer, empty baggies, stems, straws, points,
foil, and stoges. If I ever got headaches now would be the time.

A shower later…

Black Levis, black and red Airmax, Search and Destroy t-shirt,
black beanie, apathetic grey jacket—I'm reborn. *Un hombre
nuevo*. A triple-bleached needle.

Indeed! This is the last night before Slutskia comes home. One
must take advantage of such things. I pour myself a whiskey,
splash of water, and call Delancey. 'Yeah, 109 Spring…five
minutes?' and we're off

Four

Lame Lame is the latest outpost in The Meatpacking Colony.
Not so many blowjobs ago west of 9th Avenue from 14th Street to
Gansevoort was an endearing cocktail of hanging carcasses,
bloody streets and whores—lady-boy whores. Black lady-boy
whores. All this pre-photoshop of course. Entering the doors of
Lame Lame I'm accosted by the two quasi-owners. Their
inherent tragedy escapes no one but them.

'Cracula, what's up guy?'

Lord help me. We live in a special moment in our planet's
evolution. For never in all of time has their been anything more
gut wrenchingly comical than trust fund Islander kids playing
restaurateur/club owner.

'I'm fine. Where's big boy?'

'Aeronymous? He's over there. Cracula, I want to talk to you
about something.'

I'm sure you do you cunt. Instead, you should go home to the
apartment your father bought you, open all the script bottles your
uncle wrote you, down them, and jump out the fucking window.
When you've done that, send over the Midwest same same
you've been brainwashing and I'll show her how a man fucks.

'Maybe later.'

Half an hour late, I join the table. Aeronymous looks more
massive than usual. The table is of the variety bolted to the
floor, forcing the tabletop to split his mid-section, his breasts
resting on the silverware. Sporting yet another queerly florescent
BAPE sweater, it appears by the contents under the A that I've

missed the appetizer. A carpaccio of sorts. The massive oval banquet finds Fireman two sames down.

'Yo Crac, how you feeling?'

Quite alright there Fireman.

The retarded look on the two same sames bridging my boys is striking even in the world of sames. Not a day over 18, a brain cell past 1, or more than 2 weeks into the Island—they should throw in the towel. *Pronto.* Donate their organs to science, their brains to chimpanzees.

'Cracula?'

Yes Aeronymous.

'This is Re and this is Po.'

I see. To The Fireman's left are two Brazilian sames, to their left Hugatcha and Feather.

Ahh...Feather, real wife stock. Paris born, Boston raised. Not yet entered according to Aeronymous. *Could it be true?* A Princeton educated tri-lingual virgin! Five foot ten, mid-back Chinese hair, Bolivian yip white skin. A virgin? I shall indoctrinate her, open her soul. Impregnate. We shall have 500 half-bourgeois, half-Mexican natives. I'll spoon her nightly, lick her for days, only fuck her ass after marriage. I'll never force her into a threesome—unless she wants it of course. When I masturbate I'll scan through the Rolodex and finish to her. *I swear.* If she perishes before her time, I'll get FEATHER RIP over my heart. All future sames will know my only true love is gone. *Muerte.* They'll tell me they understand my detachment, the loss and all. Our mulattos will know that I'll never love another as I did you, that I'm just fucking the pain away. I will forever be a man-whore in your honor. In fact, after our 500th kid I'll have you murdered. That's how much I love you, I'll make you a martyr. Hang shrines in your honor.

Whoa…back to purgatory.

'Hey girls.' Kisses all around.

Next to Feather, Hugatcha. She possesses an ass that belongs below the Mason-Dixon and a brain too powerful for her own good. We fuck on occasion, aggressive sex — could not be hard enough for her. Must have been molested as a kid. One thing she can do, other than utilize her ass, is talk. Days on end, about whatever. Russian literature, architecture, ex-boyfriends, current boyfriend. *Lo que sea.* Quite a good resource when I've been hitting the pipe. The most compelling aspect of Hugatcha is her unshaven cunt. Principally, I'm all for Amoeban evolution in this regard. But with Hugatcha it's far from an oversight, more an indictment. A manifesto. *You shall taste me, vines and all. The Tropic of Hugatcha.* Despite hopes to the contrary, I suspect she's falling in love with me. After all, she has a boyfriend, I have a girlfriend, alcoholism, coke habit, and a bi-weekly trip to speedball island. It's a no-risk fight. The fix is in. She's fluent in Russian, but moved to Amoeba early enough to not sound like a double agent. Satan only knows what she and Slutskia banter about. I would love to imagine that in her native tongue Slutskia has more compelling thoughts on art, global warming, Amoeban foreign policy, the spread of AIDS in Africa…though doubtful. If only Hugatcha lived like she fucked (and if only Dutch girls fucked like they lived). It is what it is.

Of course Feather floats above all sames — *perhaps she's human?* In the least she's open ended. A Lynch film, a Miller diatribe, a title to a French painting — untitled. On an Island of self-appointed conclusions, she's a breath of opium filled air. An unpicked poppy field. The Golden Triangle. *Tu sabes?*

'Can I get you a drink sir?'

Indeed. Glass of red please.

'Yo Crac, you still down for the Jirque my Chain premiere this Saturday?'

Ah, he's good. The Fireman. Never a whisper, always an alpha boom for all to hear.

'Just let me know how many tickets you need. I can let my good friend He know.'

The Brazilians straighten necks, arch their backs and retort as if witnessing the second coming.

'U goey premeirey?' Hook, line, sinker. The Fireman's got you.

And in stereo: 'Yeah, He who owns Jirque my Chain is a good friend of mine.' *With sub-woofers:* 'I've given away all my tickets, but since he's a dear friend I'm sure I can get two more.'

Reel them in. I got the net.

The Fireman makes fast work of his double Grey Goose rocks. No doubt a fat bag in his pocket, couple Valiums in his belly. The man is impervious, a petrified virtuoso. A 6'4", 220-pound specimen of evolved Island imperfection. I'm afraid if he ever stopped boozing, yacking, and E dropping, he would overnight become his 40 years. Until that day he'll continue being the common denominator. From squared to square root. Taking it to the Nth to find the common link with any same in the Victoria Chiclet catalogue, or if stranded on the rings of Saturn with a bulldog dyke on dianibal, head miles below, between the (.) and the (1).

'So Crac, what'ya say?'

Sure, me plus one.

'Yo Crac?'

Yes Aeronymous.

'You down to hang for a bit after dinner?'

Perhaps Aeronymous, perhaps.

Aeronymous is a contorter. What you call a PR in Europe. His job is to twist the arms of same sames into coming to Lame Lame or similar establishments. He's quite good, working his Sidekick day and night like a six-shooter. Firing mass texts and emails, deep stuff, such as *Want a free dinner at Lame Lame tonight?* or *Are you an alcoholic? I have your fix.* His extreme girth is a blessing in the realm of contorting, being the ultimate shoulder to cry on after you've been dumped, passed over, fucked, OD'd, gone homeless, contracted the HIV, aborted your kid, had your first lesbian experience. Tragically safe. Though it must be Guantanamo Bay torture to have such proximity to young, beautiful, handicapped sames with limited consumption. I want to tell him he's not missing out. It goes on…for all the free meals consumed, he takes no part in the free alcohol—it is strictly forbidden by The Cult.

'Your drink sir.'

'Cheers. Cheers. Cheers. Cheers…'

Cheers to all you, but not before I take a sip. House red, not awful.

'Can I take your order, it's either chicken or steak. I'll start with you Aeronymous.'

'I'll take one of each. Hold the veggies.'

'Sames, for you?'

Re and Po have a look of utter confusion.

'Chicken or Steak?'

More perplexing.

'Light or dark meat sames?'

'Dark.' 'Yes Dark.' They are Danish after all.

Fireman's up. 'Sorry I don't do contorter menus' *surround sound* 'I'll take one of each app for the table and the Chilean sea bass for me. And if the sames want something else I got it.' A relentless force of nature. Unyielding.

Brazilians? 'Steakey.' Steakey.

Hugatcha? 'The chicken please. And could I get another mojito?'

Feather? 'Just vegetables.'

I love her more than ever. I shall acquire an incurable disease and eye-fuck her with it. The immaculate contraction.

'Sir for you?'

'I'll take a refill on the red and a shot of Patrón, chilled.'

'And to eat?'

Do I look hungry? I throw him a gander of my blood-shot blues.

Dinner evolves predictably. The Fireman speaks of himself and his good friends at length. '…then I took my good friend's jet to St. Tropez last year…' *front row of MSG* '…of course I always take care of him in Vegas or The Island…yeah, of course I've been to Rio, São Paolo, Angra, Búzios…my good friend…'

The Brazilians moisten in tandem, even the Danes are coming around. Aeronymous, usually charming sans timing in dinner conversation, is dead silent. After all, there's a steak to go. Despite his obvious commitment to food, his manner of consumption is far from economical. Unless he saves his clothes for later.

'Yo Aeronymous, left cheek bro.'

'Word.'

'Hey Crac, when does The Reverend get back in town?' Has The Fireman actually played the charity card? The ship's not even sinking.

'A few days I think.'

'Is he staying with you?'

'Yep.' Here we go.

'Our good friend The Reverend started his own charity in Africa helping out the poor.' *Wembley fucking Stadium* 'I'm a big donor. I figure what's the point of having all this success and money if I can't give back.'

Systems, controls, operations, conducting, managing common denominators. Fireman in action. I score another house red, chilled Patrón. Hugatcha and the future deceased mother of my 500 natives banter about, relishing in their education and superiority to the sames down the banquet. All the while envying their solace in self-objectification.

'Yo son, that shit was off the chain. Excuse me, can I get an iced coffee, extra sugar? Cracula, you wanna grab a stoge?'

Sure Aeronymous.

I throw on my apathy and make for the door.

Aeronymous slides his breasts off the table—freedom.

Marlboro lights lit, Aeronymous is off. 'Yo son, what's up with those Danish sames?'

'Re and Po? They're OK.'

'Nigga I think Po likes me son.'

Make it happen Aeronymous.

'I'm going to son. I'm gonna hit that son.'

And I'm gonna go back in, have a night cap and bid everyone farewell. Then, I'm going home to tidy up before Slutskia's arrival. Sure. 'Make it happen bro.'

'Yo son, look who it is. Hey Slave. Hey Treimee.'

Coming through customs is Slave Carsons and Treimee.

Slave is a relentlessly present fellow closing in on 40, with an Amoeban hairline to validate. A son through and through. Born in South Africa to wealthy parents, he's attempted to morph into a downtown scenester. All the while falling back on the predictable trust fund and flaunting his 3000-square-foot place in Nolita. He's the annoying sort of fellow that brings sames back to his loft and busts out the martin acoustic. For covers! I could never surmise if Slave wants to be me, or blow me. There are much better folks to be, or blow. *Lo que sea.*

'Hey Cracula, what's happening?' A real pleading son of a bitch.

And then there's Treimee. An attractive by-product of Amoeban imperialism and Cold War politics. A lovely same, though cursed with the pattern of boozing to oblivion and alerting the world. During climax, she reverts to her native tongue and shares none of Hugatcha's mission statements. 'Ohhhmygawd Craculaaa, you missed the best parteeey last night.'

Let me guess. You ran into each and every bastard that you see every other night, listened to Top 40 Hip Hop with five Classic Rock songs thrown in and ripped rails.

'It was soooo amazing. I got soooo drunk.'

Palabra.

Slave mad dogs my cock, thinking of something to say. 'When does Slutskia come back?'

I bet you'd like to know, you cunt. 'Tomorrow, Slave. Tomorrow.'

'See you guys inside.'

'Yo Cracula, that nigga's your son.'

Five

We grab the sames and head to the downstairs of Lame Lame.

Walking through the velvet rope holds no connotation as it did even six years ago. These days anyone that befriends a contorter, has a fat wallet, or not too fat a cunt, is ushered in.

'Cracula, what's up my man?'

Just preparing for another premeditated few hours.

'That's good to hear.'

Doormen, security—mad love as they say.

Aeronymous hovers. A hovering BAPE. Fireman holds up the rear, letting the sames in. Chivalric. Frivolous.

Walking down the stairs, Ligga-man blasts.

♫*You're now controlled by the motherfuckin paidest* ♫

With the contrived route Hip Hop has taken, the nightlife playlist on repeat and the chain swaggering offspring floating about, Lay-Z remains relatively digestible.

♫*Blast the propaganda in the headphones*♫

Don't get me wrong, it's no Geto Boys.

♫*If ya feelin like payin a nigga, go and get yo loot out* ♫
♫*Ladies is paid too, go and get yo loot out.*♫
♫*Anyone with cash baby, I'm telling you to.*♫
♫*Get, that, loot out yo pocket*♫

Repeater Funney art occupies the stairway. Michelangelo leads us to our table, Lay keeps spitting.

♫*I dumbed it down for all* ♫
♫*Now I got control over ya'll* ♫

The Island turning genius into bubblegum empires.

♫*All the inventors be hatin, on the loot that I'm makin*♫

The sames find their place: the Brazilians reflexively go into an ass-shaking ritual, the Danes look around for rappers, Hugatcha talks, Feather listens.

♫*Get, that, loot out yo pocket*♫

Fireman and I post up on the banquette.

'What's up Crac, you alright?'

The stance taken: paternal.
Fighting style written: friend to all.

'I don't know what you're going through brother, but I'm your friend. Let me know if you wanna talk.'

I'm not going through anything, just witnessing the decline. My decline, your decline. The Island's decline.

When our paths first crossed The Fireman was a trainee, a proby. I've witnessed his rise to Island Fire Chief. Ladder after ladder, soaring to a steady decline.

♫*Get, that, loot out yo pocket*♫

Did I want to talk? And whatever shall we converse about sir? About the time you took Tambourine, the only same I've dated that approaches humanity, on a ladder climbing expedition a month after we split up? Oh you found that common denominator. Didn't need a calculator for that one. *You call me your brother?* Our blood types aren't compatible. You play the universal donor, but you're just building up your blood bank. All that ladder dwelling, name bombing, same brain washing— and all you've to show is a house of cards.

'Nah, I don't feel like talking.'

Aeronymous sweats wildebeest pellets, frantically trying to wave down the *camarero,* steak juice settled over his face and upper BAPE. Flailing his arms he's a one-man glow in the dark rhino minstrel show. Eventually the waitress arrives with a bottle of contorter vodka, bucket of ice, false juice.

'Excuse me,' roars The Fireman, speaking for the sames, 'I'll take a bottle of Grey Goose, I can't drink that.'

Jirque my Chain premiere, name rockets, bottle orderings— Fireman doing it. He hands over his black Amex like a Pamplonian bullfighter, going for the kill.

With Lame Lame approaching capacity (shocking a place this size has the capacity for so many cunts), the DJ drops more Top 40 and all the same sames, contorters, japs, male models dressed like gangsters, and AARP members throw their hands in the air. Oblivious.

'Yo Cracula, just spoke with Lousifer, he's walking in now.' Aeronymous, my personal NPR. My Anderson Snooper. The man has a LoJack on every Islander.

'Cool.'

Grey Goose arrival. The formula's given.

'Yo Crac, what's up my nigga?'

'Chillin Lous, what's up with you?'

'Ah, whatever man.'

'No doubt, heard you had to handle some shit last night.'

'Whatever, just some nigga that robbed me. Who was puttin that on blast?'

'Who do you think?'

Laughs all around.

'That's Aeronymous for you.'

Palabra.

Lousifer makes his way through our crew for the requisite pounds, kiss-kiss, gangsta hugs, handshake.

'Yeah, I ran into this nigga, fucked him up, whatever. You partyin?'

'Still kinda going from last night.'

'Word, I got some ish if you're down.'

'Indeed kind sir, let's do this.'

'Nah, gimme your hand.'

Yeah?

'Keep that.'

Lousifer, a generous motherfucker. Off to the stall it is...

The line is five deep. Urinals occupied. Never much eye contact in the land of impending yakdom.

*Cracula! Where you been hiding? What parties you doing these days...*I'm throwing the opening of your mother's ass, piss off...*Cracula, hey man. I left you a message...*I know...*Cracula, you got any coke...*for a same I fucked five years ago? goodbye...

Alas, my stall awaits.

Now some folks are sticklers for pouring their gear out on the toilet back and chopping up a line or four. I find those bastards vile. *A club toilet seat?* When I'm rig-less, I much prefer the freckle an inch and a half southwest of my right index finger.

Fortunately, and not so, Lousifer has provided me with a rock. I search my pockets for two quarters, dimes, nickels, pesos. I've a single 1980 penny, the year of my birth. *A sign?* Divine intervention? A random visit from his holiness? Or was this penny going to attempt a blabbering session? Being the same age and all. *I ought to look in the mirror, meditate on what's happening in my world. Think about where I'm at, where I'm going.*

Fortunately, there are no mirrors in the stall. Penny and the wall will have to work. Couple or ten rips later...back to my banquet cell.

Hey Cracula, how you been? I want to talk to you about this
business opportunity. When's a good time? Let's have lunch...
Hey baby...where you been? You partying...
Yo man, what're you doing tomorrow...
Cracula, my brother? Love you bro. Call me...
There he is. Why didn't you come to my party the other night? I
rented the suite at the Royalton...
Yo, you going to Trouble Heaven later? Hunglow...
Hey bro, I'm gonna bang some D later. You down...

'For sure, hit you around three.'

'Crac, what the fuck happened to you the other night?'

It's Toreup. Her name is Tore, but there are two 5'11", blonde,
blue-eyed, ghost-skinned, nighttime Island dwelling sames
named Tore. This Tore's coping method is the yip. The other
Tore? Well, we call her Toredown.

'Who knows. Come chill with us.'

I had a thing with Toreup a few years ago, many Islanders have.
Despite (well...not despite) her cracking ways she has a place in
my heart. She's stayed with me post-Cult Camp three times, I
know her family. She's invariably dating one of my friends.

'Maybe, who you with?' *Puta.*

Back in my cell, life carries on.

The Fireman lets the Brazilians know they always have a place
to stay, if need be. 'I'm your friend.'

The Danes found the only two brothers in the joint. 'He looks
like 50 Cent.'

Treimee drank, and drank. 'I'm soooo drunk.'

Slave leans on the rail, mouth open. Stares at my cock.

Hugatcha shakes her vaginal decree, chats.

Feather sways heavenly, playing the fodder.

Aeronymous waddles in place, defying physics. He's managed to lick away the steak juice from the left quadrant of his face. A steak juice Indian. Without breaking stride, he delivers the night's final JFK greeting.

everyone jostling, positioning

seeking definition thru proximity in the symbiotic merry-go-round of interchangeable masturbation partners

adrift

those born poor, rich, molested, baptized, privileged, ostracized, illegal, addicted, afflicted, outlawed, destined, political

mistaking juxtaposition for legitimacy

Six

Content with our Aeronymous altruism, Fireman and I decide to head over to Trouble Heaven.

Trouble Heaven is one of Lark Taker's places, and I'm always up for seeing Lark. On the two-block journey The Fireman attempts a moment.

'Cracula, you know what you need to do?'

No Fireman, but I'll bet the farm you do.

'Just take it easy on the stuff. Listen, we all party. I'm not saying don't party. Just no late nights, I mean when's the last time you got laid at seven in the morning? If it's going to happen it would have happened by then.'

Has he grown so large he can only see himself? In everyone?

'With guys like us, it's hard. So many options...'

Having reached our common denominator in his head years ago, it's no use explaining I'm more letter than number.

'...and you have Slutskia coming home tomorrow. Don't fuck it up, she's a good same.'

No? When I do, won't you save her? Give her money, take her on a ladder climbing expedition. 'I hear you man, I hear you.'

Trouble Heaven is a battlefield. Repute with landmines, name-grenades, good friends, inventors, vampires.

*Kiss kiss…where you been…I tried calling
you…Cracula…what's up bro…Kiss kiss.*

Eye aversions, head nods. To the left sits a table of inventors,
name-grenade launchers and their sames.

Inventors are indigenous to The Island. They take many
shapes—entrepreneurs, financiers, DJ's, photographers,
designers, hoteliers, pop stars, students, club owners, socialites,
humanitarians, gallerists, world travelers. They are all these
things. Of course, they are none of them. The only thing they
are is arm's reach of daddy's pacifier.

At the next table sit Edison, Einstein, and Tesla—photographer,
DJ, designer. Despite daddy's millions they never pay for a
drink. They are downtown scenesters after all, they have rights.
Closing out the table are six sames of the moment, Sour, and
Sebetter.

Sour owns a place around the corner that midwives
advertisements, pop photography, referencers playing artist, the
occasional charity wank.

Sebetter is a contorter, though he swears to the contrary. He
passes his time cruising samesame.com, doing maintenance on
his contacts, calling his sponsors, and co-signers brother.

Edison, Einstein, Tesla, Sour, and Sebetter play their music. The
sames groupie along.

'Yeah, Cantbe is a good friend of mine, really sweet guy. I can
introduce you if you want.'

'They've all shown at my gallery, they wouldn't do it anywhere
else.'

The sames have no idea they're listening to covers.

'Hey Cracula, what's up with Fireman? He's a funny guy, huh?'

And you're not Sebetter?

'Hey Cracula, that Sebetter's really changed.'

And you haven't Fireman? The only brothers in the place pass each other without a word.

At the next table sits Lark's partner, Heftey Hah. Heftey has the capacity for doublecrossing, backstabbing, nuclear name-dropping, landmine laying, and Biblically lecherous lying. He can also soul search, explore, adapt, be unwaveringly loyal, and hunt the truth. Lovable, forgivable.

Heftey sits at his throne flanked by cronies, yes men, no men, inventors, sames. Plots are hatched, battle plans drawn, kingdoms divided. *Are you partying?* Stalls are breached.

Each table a sycophantic homophone.

A poor man's UN full of Amoebans, Parisians, Russians, Ukraines, Brazilians, Brits, Germans, Dutch, Mexicans, Argentines, Icelandics, Australians, Swedes, Canadians, Peruvians, Japanese, Somalians, Dominicans, Norweigans.

The melting pot of homogenous thought.

I bump into my boy Sohi. 'Cracula, what's up bro? How'd the other night end up?'

'Ah, you know how it is.'

'That I do. You coming to our show tomorrow?'

Sohi is in an all-Israeli death metal band, Pavilion. Quite good.

'Where?'

'Pianos.'

Sure, I like Pianos. The upstairs stall is the first place I tasted Dulce after all. 'No doubt.'

'If you're partyin I got.'

'I'm all supplied, thanks homey.'

'Cracula!' Carowine? 'Where yuu bin stranger?'

Carowine was a passing phase a year back or so. We boozed, got loaded, had reasonably nice sex for a few weeks. Month maybe. She hails from Eureka Springs, Tarkansas, and speaks like it.

'I tried callin yuuu.'

You know how it is.

Carowine has massive breasts, the fullest lips my cock has tasted, and record-setting elasticity of the labia. She could slingshot children over the English Channel, capture flies, open a roast beef company. I suppose it had been fun.

'Hey Carowine, how are you sweetie?' The Fireman imposes himself: kiss-kiss, paw on the DMZ between hip and ass. Rubbing. Fondling. Inflicting his formula.

Carowine informs me that I'm missed and that she's seeing Vapid Brain. Vapid is a sword swallower, blackjack dealer, box sitter. A magician of sorts.

'Are uu parteein?'

Party. Party. Party. Party. Party. Party. Party. Party. Party. Party. Party. Party. Party. Party. Party. Party. Party. Party.

I can't recall the last time I *partied*. Does one party in the hospital? The loony bin? No, one has his mouth held open, nose squeezed. One is strapped down and fed intravenously. One keeps to a schedule. One applies formulas. Proven formulas.

'Of course, let's go.'

I lead Carowine to the stall. We party.

Exiting stall left, I'm saucer-eyed. Seeing aliens. I forge my way to Lark's table in the back, Carowine trailing like a geeked gerbil. Not shockingly, The Fireman has positioned himself between two non-English speaking sames.

'Crac, what's up my love?' Kiss-Kiss. Lark is on a roll, in his element. Manifesting his creation. The (pirate)ship's captain. 'You know Tricky right?'

Tricky is a half-wit Hungarian that speaks of peace, love, and Buddhism. And there is nothing more tragic than an Islander Buddhist!

Hey Tricky. Kiss-Kiss. 'Lark, this is Carowine.' *I wonder how her lips fit in those jeans.* Kiss-Kiss. I accept my fate and sit next to Tricky.

'It's like I was telling you the other night at Hunglow. Buddhism is all about love, loving yourself, loving the earth, loving your fellow man. It's about being happy alone.'

Tricky is never a day without a 'serious' boyfriend, invariably an inventor or pop star.

'And there are no judgements on drinking, drugs, sex…'

How convenient.

'…you know what you should do?'

I am a screen. The world a projector.

'You should come with me to one of the seminars. They're right down the street from you.'

The reels are getting worse.

I drink Grey Goose, light a red, order a shot of chilled Patrón, return to the stall, find my freckle, and get started.

Pissing, I scratch my balls and am reminded of the impending Slutskia. I suppose I miss her. Do I? *Does it matter?* I could call Dulce. Carowine is here. I could order a girl off headslist. I could get head from a fat same and feel her tits. I could slam some D at Noddy's.

Outside the stall I come across Flow.

'What's happenin bro?'

El mismo.

'Take this my brother.'

Good old Flow. Thank God he broke his neck last year—endless Vicodin. I pop three.

Back on the dark side of the moon, the earth continues to revolve. *It's all about love...if you're sure you can make it, I'll ask my good friend for more tickets...hello love...*I was never a prouder Mexican.

Carowine and I jump on my flying saucer and fly threw Trouble Heaven—past the landmines, name-grenades, inventors, ladder dwellers, same sames.

The yack, Vicodin, gallons of alcohol, and lack of sleep have rendered me a wobbling wreck.

'Where to?'

'I'm stayin at a freends just down the streeyt.'

Carowine is forever staying with a friend, crashing a couch. *Lo que sea,* I'm wasted. We hop a cab.

'Thirtanth and Fifth pleayse.'

Kissing her neck and squeezing her nipples I wonder if the labia has lengthened. *How does she ride a bicycle?* No matter, we arrive.

Pleasant enough building, doorman and all. She puts a key in, hits PH1. I lay my forehead against the doors, pass out for 20 flights and come to with my face on the floor. Carowine cackles a hick laugh.

'You OKAY?'

Don't feel a thing.

'I'm gunna stay heeere fir uwhile til I git a place.'

Word.

I zombie past a small office on the left, kitchen to the right, into a decent sized living room. Already a day or two past my normal paranoia, I lay out four serpent-sized lines on the table, light an Amoeban Spirit, and feel up the block from normal.

Serpents consumed, Carowine is off to the races. Twang and all.

'Back in Eureka Springs, Tarkansas…'

Oh no.

'…when I wus twelve…'

A run-away '85 tractor trailer.

'…my uncle Otis was babysittin meey…'

'Hey babe, why don't we not talk for a minute.'

I pull out two Xanbars, crush them up with an expired credit card, make her do a line. Dumping out more gack, I combine forces and do a line, five.

Mierda!

I am on the express line—heading uptown, heading downtown. Stuck in place. Carowine appears to have left Otis and returned to The Island. She takes her shirt off and sits on my lap.

'You OKAY Cracula?'

Sure, why not. 'Whose place is this anyway?'

She mumbles something as she takes off my belt, unbuttons my jeans, and pulls out my cock.

'Whose?'

Response muffled. *Lo que sea.* I take my shirt off, try and enjoy myself. Eyes closed, I toss my head back. *Slutskia, what to do? Dulce, can I go without? The yack, does it ever end? I haven't slammed in a couple weeks, that counts for something.*

I swear Carowine must have learned to give head via bad porn. Or Uncle Otis. About to tell her to stop, I open my eyes and take in a mural of sorts on the ceiling. Squinting my saucers it comes into focus. Covering the entirety of the ceiling is an amateur rendering of Vapid Brain with his shirt off, surrounded by sames.

'Hey Car, why is there a mural of Vapid Brain on the ceiling?'

No response. I grab my base, remove it from the metronome, and pose the same question.

'Well...uh...this is his place.'

I'm up. 'What!' After all, there is honor amongst thieves, vampires, box sitters.

'Listen Cracula,' squeezing my tip, 'he's out of town.'

'Come on Car, that's not cool. You should have told me.'

Tip squeeze, base stroke.

'Sorry.' She went back to work on me. Otis.

One should never make important decisions with heightened pupils or an inflamed cock, *but when else can you?*

That said, this just isn't kosher. I have no issue with this cat, bad mural or not. But what the hell, I'll let the metronome carry on a few more minutes while I rationalize.

As Carowine pendulates I take a ganders of the place. There are pictures of Vapid everywhere. *Oh are there pictures.* Pictures of Vapid and the British PM Telme Where, pictures of Vapid and President Lush, Mandela, Michael Jackson, Spielberg, Clinton, Chirac, Schroeder, David Hasselhoff.

There is an entire wall of Vapid and tragic Hollywood types. Vapid and Bad Split, Koko Leaves, Preachin Tawke, Son Revoltcha…you've got to be kidding me.

The metronome doesn't miss a beat.

Taking it in, my position changes. Fuck this guy! Vampires, box sitters, or not.

I find myself at The Island's core. The projection of an Island dream, in the middle of a living brand. I feel nauseous.

Oh, I will show them! I pull the metronome from my cock, rip a few more blasts, and head to the bedroom, Vapid Brain's bedroom. We disrobe and mount his queen-sized bed. Two dogs intersecting each other labiaorously. Carowine facing the pillow, my ass facing the window.

Rhythmically glancing up, I notice Vapid's last picture—an image of him and Jesus in a box! Looking at the two of them, I pick up the pace.

Tripping off my speedball for kids, something starts bubbling above Carowine's ass. Thrusting on, I see The Island in her back. All the inventors are there—Edison, Tesla, Einstein, Bell, Sour, Sebetter, Slutskia…they are singular, one cell—an amoeba. Never one to pass up a good trip, I pull out and move north.

The Island unleashes a single-celled yelp, turns her head to look at me. Fishhooked! *How could I do this to her?*

Having sodomized The Island, I collapse.

estaba soñando

I was in a Delancey town car on the way to The Meatpacking. I was to meet up with Satan and God at one of Lark's places, Notice.

Arriving, I passed the rope, through the door. The clock struck midnight. It was Thursday, the place slammed. Hank was expecting me at the host stand.

'Hey Cracula.'

Hank.

'Satan's waiting for you on table three.'

Cool.

I slithered through the crowd, up the platform steps, and introduced myself.

satan, i'm cracula.

He was a handsome devil. Satan's trim 6'3" frame covered by a grey and white Gilley's t-shirt, tight black jeans, black boots and a black jacket. His hair shoulder length and curly. Guadalajara skin, green eyes. If I was healthier, we could pass for brothers. He rose.

'Cracula, I feel like we've met before.' We shook hands.

yeah?

'That after-hours on Canal maybe?'

you know, i have seen you around some late night spots.
Brownies, Vinyl, my loft.

Releasing hands, we shared a moment. He smiled a devilish
grin.

hey satan, where's god?

'Don't worry about him, never on time. I've just learned to
accept it. Hell, if I sat around waiting on him hand and foot like
everyone else, I'd get nothing done. Are you fine with
whiskey?'

sure satan. The waitress was hailed.

'Hey Satan.' kiss-kiss 'The usual?'

'Yes babe.'

This Satan was a cool cat.

'So Cracula, it's like this. God and I have a drink now and
again, talk about the old times, the future, look at chicks. That
sort of thing.'

Bottle of Jack arrives.
Cheers.
Salud.

'As it turns out, we've both developed more than a passing
interest in your evolution. This happens every few years or so.
When it does we bring the young soul along for a night of
cavorting. Speaking of, would you like a line?'

Indeed

Walking to the stall he continued. 'You see, God and I are songwriting partners of sorts. He does his bit, I do mine. Over the years we've developed a brilliant but fragile chemistry. And believe me, no one wants that chemistry upset, makes for bad music.'

Joining me in the stall, Satan pulls out a gold cigarette case and slides the top open, revealing an endless supply. Grasping the bag with his left hand, he emits a talon from his right pinky.

'So when it appears we've a common interest, an infatuation let's say, as we do with you, we make a night of it and let nature take its course.'

That's lovely Satan, not stepping on each other's toes, mutual respect, playing your bit and all...now share the goddamn bag! For the love of God!

'Oh, I'm sorry Cracula. All this stall talk and I forgot why we're here.'

Jesus Christ, come on with it.

Satan let go of the bag, leaving it levitating between us. Our fangs lengthened, eyes darkened. No Blue, No Green. Probing the eternity of the bag with his talon he presented me with a wafer of coke.

'Take this my son.'

Extending my tongue, he placed the wafer on it and met my eyes. dead silence. volumes written. It was the best yack I'd ever done. *How nice would it be to slam?*

'We can do that later. Trust me, God won't be up.'

We slithered our way back to the table. Satan and I.

'I see God's finally showed. Allow me to introduce you.'

Slumped over our table was a fellow wearing a beat-up sweater, his forehead resting on the table, enshrouded in blonde locks.

'God, God, hey God...wake up.' Satan tapped his shoulder. 'God meet Cracula.'

Leaning back, God revealed a Daniel Johnston t-shirt under his open sweater, littered with burn holes. 'Cracula, it's nice to finally meet you.' God was unshaven, his blue eyes pinned. He cast his flags on my saucers for a moment, then nodded off. I wondered if he was alright.

'Oh don't worry, he does this all the time, nodding off in public. I'm half-surprised he even showed. Another drink?'

Sure Satan.
Cheers.
Salud.

'You know Cracula, I still love visiting The Island. It's nothing like it used to be, so damn sanitary these days. Formulaic really.'

satan, i hear ya.

'I can't recall the last time God and I hooked up in The Island, or Amoeba for that matter. The 40s maybe? When I come now it's alone, for a good laugh.'

Satan, comedy fan?

'Oh I'm a sucker for unwitting stand-up.'

God surfaced from his nod. 'Satan, would you ask the waitress for a nice bottle of red, nothing too extravagant.'

'Sure God.' Satan leaned in, whispered. 'He used to be much more affable, God. Always sipping wine, water. Then one day he saw me slamming the D and became curious. He badgered me for years, centuries really—*come on Satan, fix me Satan, just this once Satan.* Not wanting to upset our chemistry, I invariably turned him away. Finally, his begging curiosity became so pathetic our chemistry was already screwed—so I turned him on. Unfortunately, he got turned out. Then again, I think the clever bastard may have been playing me the whole time. Now that he's cultivated a habit, he receives loads of empathy. You know what I mean?'

I do Satan.

'And when he does finally pay a visit, stick to a speaking engagement, join a dream...everyone's so dumbfounded they pay ever so close attention. Clever junkie that God.'

God lit a stoge and nodded off.

'Where were we my young Cracula? Ah yes, the impending comedy show. Tomorrow night's another one of those asinine group masturbations at The Garden.'

That's right.

'You know the ones. All the big Amoeban bands at the time get together, play their music and yell *Down with the President...Fuck the war...We need to love each other...*It's by far the most narcissistic, predictable and superfluous collection of emotions I have the pleasure of witnessing every 20 years or so. Even more bellyache laugh tragic are the groupies that flock to these circle jerks—inventors, ladder dwellers, super sames, humanitarians. And the illest? HA! Look to your right.'

Glancing over I see actors, Hollywood actors. Bambalina Holierthanthee, Rat Billin, Wrong Choose, Trickless Sage, Unkeen Remix, Preachin Talke, Monny Repp, Bad Fit, Jorge Looney, Playafor Buxx, Spearya Lightley.

'These are my creation, Hollywood actors.'

Satan took a moment to light a red, reflect, giggle. He seemed proud of himself.

'Cracula, wow! Have you ever seen anything more hilarious? Like I was telling you, God and I do our best to remain in synch, but now and again it's just not working and we do our own thing for a bit. The last solo break I had went to these jesters. More of a long-term investment for when things get slow. I had no idea the centuries of laughs I'd spawned, if for no one else but me.

'These people pass themselves off as artists! HA! They speak of creation! HA! They've no idea they're billboards, editorials, advertisements. They pass being a spokesmodel for another's art as art itself. They recite others' words, wear others' makeup, pose in front of others' cameras. Bask in false lighting. They receive awards and admiration for pretending to be another human that *was* great! They are reassured, revered and blown, for mimicking unique souls! Goddamn karaoke singers. HA!'

Satan was an insightful dude.

'It wasn't enough for them to butcher others' words, visions, stories. Oh no! They had to co-opt entire lives.'

Satan let out a Miltonian laugh so piercing God came to and sipped his wine. I lit another red and pounded whiskey.

'Cracula the best part of it is, they are oblivious.'

Oblivious, my favorite *palabra*.

'Is it? That one's mine.'

yours?

'Yeah, the English language is split 50/50. God made a word, I made a word. God. Me. Of course our offspring have bastardized and added through the years, but yeah, oblivious was mine.'

Was every language conceived like this?

'No, reluctantly I let him have the rest. Except German.'

Dankeschoen.

'*De nada* Cracula.'

but what about Gary Oldman, Mickey Rourke?

'Goddamn Cracula, I love you more every drink. A few years ago I actually felt sorry for these Hollywood jesters—their lack of awareness. I took out time from my busy schedule and went door to door to let them in on their plight, command them to quit doing biopics. But no one was home! The bastards were all doing yoga or listening to Radiohead. Hey, what are you gonna do? The only two cats that would have a drink with me? Gary and Mickey. Great guys, solid souls.

'Groupies aside, the main attractions for tomorrow's comedy circus are to your right.'

Lighting a red and pouring another whiskey I viewed the crowd.
The Amoeban bands were all there—Pun Jam, Sound Slave, The
Dead Hots, The Jokes, Rue Too, Tepid Evolver, Fade Into The
Machine—littered with same sames, inventors, ladder dwellers,
Sour, Sebetter, sycophants.

The singer of the Dead Hots was flanked by 15-year-old sames.
He carried on about his higher power—unaware God was in the
room. *Oblivious*. The Jokes boozed alone, reveling in their
attire. The guitar players from Rue Too and Sound Slave spoke
textbooks, politics, nonsense. Tepid Evolver lit stoges, drank
whiskey, water.

At the table next to us sat Beddie Wetter and Bozo. They waxed
literature, philosophy, the infinite. Congratulated each other on
being world leaders.

God took a sip of vino, re-lit his smoke, and nodded off. Satan
presented another wafer.

'Now all these guys, these musicians, were a joint creation
between God and I. He wrote his bit, I wrote mine. Cracula, it's
like a chess match. I make my move, but anticipating his next
five. There've been times we've finished entire civilizations in a
day. These fellows here are much more complex. They took
ages, as did you.'

God nodded in approval.

'God would invent a trait, I would counter. He would counter
my counter. This went on for lifetimes. Eventually you just
move on.'

Wafer taking effect, paranoia set in. God spoke.

'Just because you're paranoid, don't mean they're not after you.'

thanks god

'What's left is a beautiful mess. Living, breathing conundrums. Past all the addictions, the insanity, pride, self-righteousness, need to be worshipped, idol speak, womanizing, hypocrisy, isolating, projected detachment, manic-depression, self-worth, narcissism. Past all those things, at the core of these fellows are two things. The ability for truth and a preacher's ego.'

is that right satan?

'Of course it is, therein lies the conundrum. Possessing the rarest of abilities, recognizing truth, yet only able to preach to the choir.'

Satan ripped a prideful laugh. God nodded.

'They are gatherers of many, converters of fuck all. Why do you think these circle-jerk comedy shows always take place in The Island or Lost Aimless. The audience is the choir, is the donor, is the critic, is the derivation, is the lover, is the co-signer, is their God. HA! Now there are a few truthful poets lacking a preacher's ego, but they only grasp their truth, not universal truth. And the one who held it all? Well, you know where he sits.'

well i'll be damned satan.

'Probably, but the night is young.'

Not sure if it was the paranoia of the second wafer or my usual delirium, but I heard a far off *Cracula wake up*. It rang with a southern accent.

Cracula, someone's heere.

No shit. Satan, God, Beddie, Bozo. Where you been? a more emboldened whisper. *Damn it Cracula, wake up!*

Seven

Coming to, Carowine is hovering six inches from my face, a finger over her mouth.

'Goddamn it Car I was having a sick dream! I'm going back in.'

Painful whisper. 'Someone's heere.'

'What?'

'Someone's heere.'

'I thought dude was gone?'

'He eeys, it's one of his freeends.'

Here we go.

'He's eeyn the office, on the compuuuter. But I thank he's just heeere to check on meey.'

Can't imagine why. Where's Satan when I need him.

'And Cracula, he's inormous. Looks like a damn wrastler.'

Fucking hell.

This is what I get. Should have left and avoided karma. No fuck that! Fuck Vapid. That mural, those pictures. Jesus in a box! And fuck this brute in the other room.

Rolling off the bed, away from the door, I dress quickly. Precisely. Measuring my breaths. I'll wait it out, Carowine just has to keep him at bay.

Skull throbbing, endorphins play catch with my limbic system. Fangs grow. The brute booms:

'CAROWINE, CAN I COME IN THERE A SECOND? VAPID WANTS ME TO GET SOMETHING.'

I reach for my shank.

'Eeyn a meeynit, I need to geeyt dressed.'

My shank? Back pockets, front pockets. Fuck, must have left it in the cab. I'm not sure if this predicament has anything to do with Satan or God, but it's damn sure a conundrum and I'm in the wrong, mural or no.

I freeze for a minute, contemplate the move. Neurons slowly come to life, testosterone returns. Fangs full of venom.

Stepping out of my body, I see myself fetaled on the floor. *Fuck this!* Let's get on with it.

I rise up, march to the bedroom door. Carowine whispers, 'Cracula, no.' No matter, I'll take her down with the ship. The inevitability of right and wrong can find me later.

I open the door as a mute kamikaze, a venerable silent film cowboy. Fists drawn, chest out, blue eyes wide. *Alas,* the enemy is nowhere in sight. Carowine lurks behind, a parasite. Antennae extended, I sense the OGRE looming in the office, near my escape route. I tiptoe a Marine step towards the escape hatch and reach my left hand for the safety portal, right fist cocked—adrenal system a go. Opening the gate, I catch wind of the sloth's back. IMMENSE.

I don't bother closing the portal and sprint down the 20 flights, laughing hysterically. Not a care in the world.

Eight

Paying the cabbie, I light another red and climb my stairs. I can't recall the last time I slept. *Have I slept?* Satan. God. Sodomy.

It's been years since I could separate what was dream, reality.

Pulse?

Is Slutskia coming home today? She is. I should probably clean the place. Throw out the stems, baggies, rigs. Do the dishes, change the sheets. This is her home too after all. Should I order flowers, candy? Borscht? I should, but that can wait. I need sleep. I need a parachute.

Quite strategically, I planned for this exact moment a few days or so ago. Noddy and I were having a speedball session and I covertly loaded a point, sans yack. Where had I put it? Oh yeah, Ziplock bag next to the Frosted Flakes.

Ziplock unzipped, I wrap my belt and pump my fist. Unlike Noddy, my veins still present a plethora of options. *After all, I'm no damn junkie.*

Right arm, lower Broadway. I wiggle the tip in, strike gold, pull out some DNA, and slam it back in…

Fucking hell.

Blues pinned, I cap the rig and scratch my temple. Pouring a bowl of cereal I think of nothing.

estaba soñando

I was a donkey, living and working in Santorini. My days subsisted of taking fat-ass tourists up the winding road of a mountain overlooking the bay. They were too lazy to walk. I was owned, operated, and whipped by a guy named Nikos.

My days began at sunrise, schlepping up the local supplies from the boats to the cliff's top. What a view it was. The lard-infused tourists came an hour or so later.

The Amoebans were the fattest   obese and bloated   The biggest loads, least adventurous, most hurried to reach the top. They never enjoyed the journey up, just looked forward to the view from above. Bitching the whole way—my smell, deliberate pace, bathroom breaks. They thought I was a mule for Chrissake! I'm no half-breed, save for my horse cock.

Up and down I repetitioned. Carrying lazy bastard after squishy cunt from the ocean to the mountain top. Never a thank you, just a kick in the ass.

Nikos charged 10 Euros a climb, the bastard. He fed us only once a day, oats. Never any wine to wash it down. No Ouzo, No Mythos.

Then one day I gathered my fellow donkeys and hatched a plot. An uprising, a revolution. A donkey scheme.

My fellow asses were to maintain their donkey monotony—slow trot, funky odor, occasional shit stop on the way up the mountain. I was to sneak away at night and bathe in the Mediterranean, comb my hair, get highlights. I would pluck my eyebrows, do tail raises, read *Donkey Health*.

My metamorphosis was slow, deliberate. No need to alarm
Nikos just yet. I trudged up and down the mountain, slowly
changing. Never late for work, never complaining.

Then one full-mooned night I went for it...

I took all the Kiehl's products we had confiscated and galloped
to Akrotiri, the red beach. I washed and conditioned my hair,
cleared the wax from my ears, scrubbed my donkey balls. I had
my mistress, Jackalynne, braid my mane and shave my donkey
ass.

we had donkey sex in the moonlight

After that, Jackalynne painted my saddle menstrual red and
sewed on an emblem. A moniker. My new identity.

THE MAD DONKEY

Nine

I come to.

Pain. Epic.

Removing my face from the floor, I give an attempt at recalling the past few days. What day is it? Month? *Did I do coke with Satan? With a donkey?*

The place is a fucking disaster. I need to clean, shower. Purge. I gather all the stems, baggies, rigs, porn DVDs, lubricant, beer, whiskey, empty cigarette boxes, tinfoil—throw them out.

Passing my PC, I close headslist.com and open Inert Outlook. Delete penis-lengthening creams, stock tips, hardening pills, mood stabilizers, party invites, asmallturd notices, and racebook requests. I come upon an email from The Reverend.

The Reverend, my former partner in crime, has taken it upon himself to save Africa from itself. A born-again. He's been gone two years and I miss him dearly. He was quite the roadblock to deterioration. His monthly emails, *Notes from West Africa: An Altruist's Journey,* make me proud and nauseous. Swallowing my vomit, I open the latest.

Sitting in front of a computer in Monrovia, I picture the Reverend picturing himself a combination of Hemingway, Indiana Jones, and Jane Goodall. His prose:

Dear Islanders,

I write you today as an ex-pat, a patriot nonetheless. A patriotic Christian. I can't put into words the horrors I have seen in West Africa, but with the help of Jesus I'll try.

As most of you know, I used to live in The Island. In fact, I used to live it up in The Island. Perhaps you saw me out drinking, having fun. If so, I apologize. Don't think for a minute I was enjoying myself. It was horrible and my life was going nowhere. I was simply pillaging the land. That was all before I accepted Jesus in my life.

The Lord has led me to those most in need, Liberians. I honestly don't know what they would do without me. The entire country lives without clean water, a consistent food supply, and cable TV.

For what all of you selfish bastards spend on a night on the town, I can single-handedly save ten people a day. You should all feel horrible about your lives, and you're probably going to hell. However, I have a way to save you. If you donate just $20 and accept The Lord as your savior, all is not lost.

Act swiftly and with God's mercy.

Reverend

Despite this, I'm fairly certain his heart is in the right place. If only by chance.

I jump in the shower, wash away my sins.

Ten

Two hours later I emerge a new man. *bleached* Slutskia will be home any minute. I do miss her. At least the idea of a Slutskia, the parallel existence. The possibility of a Slutskia. No, I'm sure I love her. *I wonder if she gained weight?*

I order a bottle of champagne to go along with the fresh sheets, washed hair, and shaved mug. Genuinely happy, I think.

Patiently I wait, high on anticipation, only slightly nodding. The arrival of Slutskia will change the pace of my universe—slow down a few orbits, create some moons, cause a few meteor showers. I'm not worried, nature will take its course. *I do love her.*

KNOCK KNOCK

'Baybee, open fauking door.'

Lighting a smoke, I wish her plane crashed.

'Cracula, open fauking door.'

What to do?

Communist screams: 'Baybee! Cracula!'

Accepting my sentence, I open the door. 'Hey babe.'

Slutskia throws her arms around me, crushing her DDs against my chest (to think she had a reduction).

'Baybee, I lauv you.'

Hmmm.

'U lauv me baybee? U mees me?'

Sure.

'Baybee!?'

'Yeah babe, I missed you.'

If nothing else, Slutskia is sex. Pure sex. Destined to be sex, condemned. She has Barbie locks, Aryan eyes, double agent skin, graphic breasts, an ass like a twelve-year-old boy—with Cracula tattooed above it. She is one long ego stroke. When The Island steals my identity, I can always bend her over, see my name in lights. That and we are both spics. *Tu sabes?* Oh, and she loves sames. Kissing sames, eating sames, bringing sames home for us. This last fact is often alluded to by The Fireman. *This same same is into sames, we should put them together, see what happens…she thinks Slutskia's hot, what'ya think…* What do I think? I think what kind of fellow negotiates for his good friend's same? Well, most fellows in The Island.

Arousal. It has been just long enough since our last encounter for this one to taste fresh. Similar to not drinking for a day, half day maybe. Sensing my intent, she heads for the shower.

'Baybee, I need clean my puuussy first.'

Slutskia is forever cleaning her snatch, shaving her snatch, massaging her snatch, cultivating her snatch. She takes five showers a day, an amphibious kitten.

'Baybee I jus git off plane. Savunteen-hour plane.'

I could care less. I don't mind the taste of economy, peanuts.

The showerhead comes to life.

'Hey babe?'

'Yes baybee.'

'My friend I told you about, The Reverend, he's coming to stay with us next week.'

'OK baybee.'

As she scrubs and investigates my thoughts turn to Feather. Eventually all this Dulce, Slutskia, cracking, slamming, boozing business will grow old. Everything does. Inevitably I'll want Feather, or a Feather. When that day comes, will I be too contaminated? Will I have seen too much to relate to an actual human? Probably.

'Baaaybeeee...'

Slutskia meets me on the couch, naked and whitewashed. Climbing on top of me we join as two wayward parasites, galloping through the hills and into our sunset.

Eleven

We ride out our second honeymoon for a few days, Slutskia and I. We see Hollywood movies, have worse conversation, go to the Russian bathhouse. We subject ourselves to dinners with Flow, The Fireman, Brazilian sames. Drink iced coffee with Aeronymous.

Having exhausted the exhaustive, nature takes its course.

'Baybee wake up. Cracula, wake up. CRACULA!'

'Jesus fucking Christ babe. What?'

'Baybee, power out.'

'What?'

'BAYBEE FAUKING POWER OUT!'

Rolling out of bed, I hit the light switch.

Fuck.

It's five degrees outside and I live in a one-window cavern. There is but one thing to do. I dial my landlord, knowing he won't answer.

'Sanjay, it's Cracula. There's no power in the building, I'm checking into a hotel. I'll deduct it from next month's rent.' *Babe, pack some shit.*

Now there are many ways to take a vacation without ever leaving The Island—concerts, theater, hallucinogens, Tuesday Science section of *The Times*—none as pleasant as a reckless night in a hotel. A hotel far from downtown. We pack a bag and head for The Hudson.

Out of the cab, up the escalator, to the front desk we go.

'Yes sir, how may I help you?'

'I'd like a room please, junior suite.'

'Certainly, may I have a credit card?'

Handing over my Commerce debit, it's 50/50.

'OK sir, you're in room 609, up the elevators to your left.'

Rising to our doom, Slutskia has a brain flash. 'Baybee, let's make party.'

Palabra.

There are suites and there are suites. This is neither. A den of inebriation at best. Checking my crackberry, I see a text from Dulce.

What are you doing?

This is an enormous decision. Massive. A nation's future.

Risk. Reward. Fork in the road. Dulce.

I return her text.

Hudson Hotel
Room 609

Bring yip

OK 1 hr

Needing courage, we hit the bar.

Two shots of Patrón please. Room 609.
Two more shots please. 609.
Yeah, 609.
Yes.
609.

More than buzzed and in need of coke, we return to our den.
Shall I give a quick poke? Or hold out, just in case?

DING DONG.

Expecting Dulce, I open the door. It's La Yipessa. Why is she
here? Had I texted her? Had Slutskia? No matter.

'What's up Yipessa, come in.'

She hasn't slept, geeked beyond repair. Stuttering, blabbering,
roaming—I speak her language. She sits down, presents a bag.
Would we like some? Oh would we.

Couple rips here, couple rips there…whackos everywhere.

We speak of nothing. I mostly watch La Yipessa's jaw do the
Greek alphabet, I believe she's on Omega. I keep a close watch.
This particular zippiddydooda is a goddamn klepto, always
pocketing rolled up bills, Snickers bars, socks. *Lo que sea.* I
ponder her usefulness, her utility. I channel Mill.

DING DONG.

'I got door baybee.'

Here we go.

'Hi.' Hello. 'I Cracula same same, Slutskia.' I'm Dulce.

Fuck me. 'Hey Dulce.' Cautious kiss-kiss. 'You meet Slutskia?'

'Yes,' innocent smile. Innocent my ass.

The cards are dealt.

'I brought this for us.' Dulce throws five bags on the table, big bags. Shrugs her shoulders, smiles an entrapping smile. I taste her contribution, much spicier than La Yipessa's.

Slutskia meets Dulce's eyes, revealing her intentions. A true thesbian. She glances at me, accusing. Blind. I glance at Yipessa and tune a hymn in my head. *One of these pieces is not like the other*. What shall we do?

'Sames?'

Yes.

'Would you like to play a game?'

Sure.

'OK. Well first everyone do a line.' No arm-twisting needed. 'Now, I'll spin the bottle. When it stops, you do whatever I say.'

Ha ha. OK. Sure.

'Great, it landed on stop. Slutskia, Dulce, take your shirts off.'

La Yipessa recites the Armenian alphabet. Says she's moving to
Lost Aimless with her husband and we should all come visit.
Sure. She moves on to Swahili as Dulce and Slutskia remove
tops, giggle. Slutskia's suspicion is only surpassed by her
arousal. We all do a line, Yipessa steals the remote.

As luck would have it, the bottle stops again. They kiss.
Yipessa answers her phone, it didn't ring.

We polish off bags, vodka.

On the road to destruction or creation, I'm not sure. I have that
teenage sensation of receiving fellatio with your mom in the next
room. So far so good, but there could be tears any minute.

Thus far, Dulce is sticking to the tacit script. We spin on.
Yipessa speaks to Japanese imperialists.

Slutskia and Dulce now in their panties—kissing, groping,
fondling. Yipessa speaks Latin, steals my gum.

I am an early warning volcano telegram.

With another spin of the bottle Yipessa will be extraneous. I tell
her there's an English lesson downstairs, room 86.

Panties off, inevitability unfolds. I sit back and wait my turn.
My same and mistress play Lewis and Clark for awhile, explore
the unknown.

Vesuvius warning signs posted.

They alternate pleasing each other, themselves, me. I steal
glances and back arcs—careful to keep at least one eye on
Slutskia. *Waiting for Father Time to catch up with me.*

Those in the Mount St. Helens region are told it's too late.

Squaring up with Dulce's eyes and my namesake, I move in. Careful not to disrupt an already set rhythm, the flow of nature, or melt anyone just yet. Steady. Picking up the pace now and again, I yield when fishhook is reached—wanting to keep all the troops involved.

An artificial pacemaker.

Staring at my name, I thrust Slutskia—make love to Dulce. They are a one-headed rendezvous. I tell myself I love Dulce. *Did I mouth it?*

Another fishhook and our first impasse is reached.

The sames change position—a moment of truth. Slutskia's soul meets mine, meets Dulce's head.

As I enter Candyland, Slutskia's eyes roll. Dulces's tongue straightens them out. Progressing, I attempt to manage the precarious balance floating in the air, keep my foot off the third rail. Alternating glances down toward the task at hand and empathetic shots at Slutskia, I am Kofi Annan. I shall move Dulce in with us, make this my daily chore.

We carry on.

Reaching the finish line, I break into a sprint. Alarms are sounded. Tropical storms. Tornado alerts.

Mount St. Cracula blown.

What will be the repercussions? Have I buried myself?

I disengage, leave my two Juliets to their own devices.

Admiring my work, I blast another line, six. My ego about to explode. Small talk strictly avoided, we continue. *Nothing stops progress.* Drinking. Ripping. Blasting. Eyeing. Approaching my favorite mistake.

It must be pointed out, Slutskia and I are no virgins in the land of third party sames. Within that land is kosher and non-kosher dining. I have thus far adhered to a strict diet.

Properly loaded, Slutskia and Dulce lie on the bed and please themselves, stare at each other—to my left, to my right. Having so far respected the laws of the land, I've now two choices. *Why does it feel like I'm at a Greek diner?* I know the correct selection, the *ménage a trois* PC choice.

Fortunately, I'm surfing the yip.

I rise. Skeed up, gacked. Throw Dulce's legs over my shoulders.

This could go sour. Beginning work on Dulce, Slutskia's face turns south. Masturbates. Stroking along, I've yet to walk off the cliff, publicly renounce the queen or burn the flag. Making eye contact with Dulce, I go there.

Grabbing her face, I lean in, administer a meaningful kiss.
Goddamn it

Convicted, I take a seat.

(crackberry ring)
'Fireman, what's up?'

'You'll never believe the same I met tonight.'

Yeah?

'This new Brazilian. What lips, ass, perfect little breasts. I was at my place and she walks in, the whole club stopped and she just stared right at me. I know she wants me.'

Did you talk?

'Well it was hard, she was with her mom. She can't be a day over 14, but really mature. You know when you can just tell?'

Not really.

'The body of a sixteen year-old. The way she shook her ass! Oh my god. She couldn't take her eyes off me. I know she wants me bad. That other Brazilian was there too, you know the one from Miami? She was staring at the fourteen year-old staring at me, which made her want me even more...' *Sound travels 700 mph, mach 1. Light travels 670 million mph, mach 900,000 (from Charles de Gaulle to LAX in 1/20 of a second). Cell phones exist in a speed-of-light world, which means I'm being subjected to The Fireman's masturbation **before** the sames on either side of him! Oh the suffering* '...on top of that, there was a new one, an older one. Maybe eighteen. She came right up to me and told me she wants me. And there was a whole table of Brazilians sitting across from us, and guess what? They stared at me all night! That made the entire club want me. I'm heading home now with a couple Brazilians. I would invite you over, but they want me too bad. What are you up to?'

'I got this Slutskia/Dulce thing doing.'

'Yeah? Where? I'm coming over.'

Goodbye.

(crackberry ring)
'Aeronymous, what's up?'

'Chillin son, just leaving Lame Lame. What're you doin?'

'Curing cancer.'

'Word. You wannna hit Desperanto's, grab a coffee?'

'I'm good.'

'These two slammin sames are gonna meet me there son.'

Sure.

'And they're down son. They wanna get slammed son.'

'I'll call you back.'

Crackberry again, It's Noddy.

'What up Noddy?'

Silence.

'Yo Noddy, what's up?'

Silence.

'Noddy?'

Silence. His phone drops.

Slave calls. Ignore.

Treimee, no doubt with Slave, sends a text.

I'm soooo drunk   call us

Peace.

Tambourine calls. Ignore. She follows with a text.

*Cracula, I'm sure you dialed me by accident, but Dim
and I r trying 2 sleep. This is not a very thpiritual
hour to have ur phone ring. If you'd like 2 speak at a
more appropriate hour, I'm here 4 u in ur time of need.
Thpiritually urs
Tambourine*

Oh lord. I hold back vomit, laughter. Why couldn't Feather
send a text? Satan? God? Fuck it, let's order turkey clubs and
Corona.

Slutskia and Dulce continue to occupy themselves. I'm spent,
over it. Roaming. Should I hit Noddy's? Slam some D? Could
Lousifer get?

Lous what up?

Lark sends a text.
*Hello love
R u in the mood to get naughty?*

Feeling naughtied out, I tell him I'll call later. Lousifer
responds.

What's good son?

Chillin U?

I rack up two more lines, make myself a fresh vodka. Could
these two get a fucking room? The Fireman sends three more
texts.

WHERE ARE YOU!
?
Call me

Lark
Zippity doo da zippity day

Lousifer
Getting twisto u?

Even Flow's still up.
Where u at?

I hit Lousifer back.
Got any D?

Dumping out more gack, Dulce and Slutskia come up for air.
They are in the middle of what appears to be a conversation.
Imagining the depths and revelations...

Lousifer hits me back.
No but I can get

Word.
Meet me at my place in 1 hr?

Lousifer
No doubt

The two charlatans quit talking, resume.

Ducking sharpshooters, helicopters, heat-seeking missiles,
poisonous clowns, midget ninjas, tarantulas—I get dressed.
Scooping up most of the yack, I tell the lovers I'll be right back.

My next obstacle is escaping the well-lit Hudson for the cover of an Island night. Stepping into the blinding hall I'm visually assaulted by two security guards, no doubt investigating the racket coming from room 609. *Did they recognize my face? Had I been photographed at the desk?*

I do a 180 and head toward the stairwell. They keep a healthy distance, too healthy. Must be police. I feel them slowing the pace, pushing something. Making the mistake of turning around, I see they have acquired a food cart to throw me off.

Sure they have shotguns under the white tablecloth, I begin a full sprint to the stairs — too late for stealth maneuvers.

Reaching the stairwell, I turn around and see them knocking on room 609.

'Room service.'

Remembering I ordered turkey clubs and Corona, I try and calm myself. Nevertheless, I take the stairs, end up in the storage room, come up the service elevator to street level and hail a cab.

'109 Spring please.'

The cabbie plays talk radio. Paranoia grows. Dumping on my freckle, I down another blast. The Fireman sends a text.

Call me, I met some more Brazilians...they want me!

Aeronymous
Son, should I wait for you at desperantos? The sames r down

Slutskia
Baybee wer u go

Lousifer
Where u at son?

Flying down Seventh Avenue we bust a left on Spring, pass
Rim's pizza, Dying A, Fusion, Doom, Gac Cosmetics, and stop
opposite Evolution—109 Spring. I give the cabbie a rolled up
ten.

'What up Lous?'

'What up son? You good?'

We climb the stairs and enter 3N, power back on.

'How was your night?'

'All good son. Made some money, fucked some dude up.'

Word. Word.

Of all the tangled webs I've weaved, Lousifer and I have
managed to avoid each other's. We sit spider to spider. In many
ways, he is the only real man I know. Speaks his mind, does
what he says, has no ulterior motives. I dump out the coke, he
rolls up a 100.

Blast. Off.

'I hit up Lame Lame with Aeronymous, same shit, same sames.
You?'

'Just hung out with Slutskia, saw Dulce for a minute.'

'Word?'

Yeah.

'So what's up with Dulce now that Slutskia's back? You gonna peace that out?'

Actually, I'm gonna move her in. Have two sames, go Mormon. 'Yeah, guess I have to.'

'Word. Yo I wanted to talk to you about something, and be straight with me. No matter what, be straight up with me nigga. Cool?'

Sure.

'If you're done with that, I wanna take her out.'

Come again?

'But yo, only if you're cool with it son. If not, then I won't even go there. You're my boy, I'm coming to you before I even think about it. If you mind, let me know.'

Did I mind?

Did the queen of England mind handing over the crown jewels? Would surfers give up the moon? Would any of my friends do this for me?

'Nah, I don't mind.'

What was I going to do? Say no?

Goddamn it!

At least he came to me, asked. Is there any other Islander that would have? The gods of timing must be pissing themselves.

'You sure?'

'Yeah I'm sure. You got that H?'

Lousifer hands me a vile of smack. Relocating to the couch, I dump the entirety over my freckle. Kill it.

Holding the empty vile in my left hand, I notice the warning label for the first time.

If you have been: up for days, consuming gallons of alcohol, sniffing miles of coke, or all of the above; IT IS NOT RECCOMENDED THAT YOU INHALE THIS ENTIRE VILE OF HEROIN.

The Island got quiet. The voices shut off.

Silence.

estaba soñando

I fornicated with Miller and boozed with Bukowski.
I dropped E with Irvine, I raped with Roman.

I empired with Alexander, satirized with Swift.
I toured hell with John.

I taught Rembrandt photoshop,
I gave Van Gogh a q-tip.
I did lines with Pablo and read lines with Gary.

I left the Milky Way with Stephen and hawked Kahn's spoils.
I accepted awards with Phillip, for the future I said OK Dick.

I speedballed with Jean-Michel,
I shot with William and shanked with Norman.
I rose from the south like Bill.

I lie like Ernest.

Twelve

Shock. Shock. Breathe. Nurcan.

Breathe. Breathe.

Shock.

I've nothing against police or firemen (as an Islander how can you?). But when the bastards are playing your music, flipping through your photos, and lying on your couch? While you receive Nurcan on a stretcher! Well.

Coming to, the paramedic tells me I've OD'd and to lay back and relax. OD'd? Again? Then why the hell am I in my apartment with IPD and FDI? Could I not have been brought back to life in an ambulance like usual? Or by that one gay doctor at St. Vincent's?

'Lay down, you don't wanna get up. Trust me dude.'

'Yeah?'

'Yeah homey, if you start boppin around these pigs are gonna arrest yo ass.'

Dude, homey, pigs — arrest my ass? Is this how paramedics talk these days?

'Yeah dude, your boy here saved you. You were dead homey, he gave you mouth to mouth, beat some life back into you.'

'You're not a cop right?'

'Hell no son!'

Leaning up, 'Did my boy get rid of the shit?'

'Nah, but I got here first, it's in my pocket.'

'Word?'

'Word, but you cats ain't getting it back. I got some other shit for you. What's your boy's name?'

'Lousifer.'

'Cool name. Lousifer, let's do this.'

Unable to find anything, other than a few DVDs for the station, the cops clear out. The firemen are a bit more empathetic, telling me I must have a nice fulfilling life; why am I blowing it on this shit; I should settle down, get a girl. Do I have a fire escape?

I tell them to grab a couple bottles of flavored whiskey on the way out, for the boys.

The paramedic wheels me through my loft, towards the stairs. I realize that after dying, reviving, vomiting, and Nurcan influx...I'm much more sober than Lousifer. *How had he maintained composure around the cops?* Geeked! Given me mouth to mouth. Dulce? Hell, take Slutskia too.

As the paramedic and his partner carry me out, I sniff a familiar fragrance. Opening my eyes we come upon Slutskia and Dulce walking up the stairs.

'Baybee, what da fauk!'

She looks genuinely perplexed (shocker). A satisfied Dulce looks over her shoulder, shrugging innocently. They do look good together.

'Don't worry babe, just a formality. The power's back on.'

Never ones to stop the party, the two sames go upstairs to do god knows what. Levitating out of my building I see The Fireman and Aeronymous by the ambulance.

'Hey Crac, these are my good friends Brazil Samey and Brazil Same Samey. Listen brother, if you need to talk I'm here for you. Slutskia's probably having a hard time right now, I'm gonna go check on her.'

Thanks Fireman.

'Cracula, I know now's not the time...'

Do you?

'But there is a better way. You really need to join The Cult. There's a Cult meeting tonight if you wanna go. Call me after St. Vincent's.'

He leans in, whispers.

'I would go to the hospital, but I gotta get these two Brazilo sames' numbers.'

Thanks Aeronymous.

I see Tambourine, she's there in thpirit. 'Cracula, take these crystals. They were blessed by a shaman healer on Bleecker.'

Thanks Tambourine.

Fireman, Aeronymous, and the two sames trot up the stairs. Tambourine breaks into a chant and vanishes. Lousifer boards the ambulance with me. *Must he have revived me?*

'So check it out, I gotta throw away the gear fellas. You're lucky I snatched it before the cops showed. You cats'd be high *and* locked up, and that's a *real* motherfucker. And listen, I party, lord *knows* I party, but you gotta take it easy. Make sure you get good shit.'

Lousifer chimes in.

'I usually do.'

'Word, lemme get your number.'

'No doubt son.' 'Word.' 'Word up.' Word.

They exchange numbers, speak of mutual friends, late night spots.

'And what's your name?'

Cracula.

'I'm gonna leave you with some fresh needles and Nurcan. Keep this shit close by when you're partying. You gotta party safe homey.'

PARTY. PARTY. PARTY. PARTY. PARTY. PARTY. PARTY. PARTY. PARTY. PARTY. PARTY. PARTY. PARTY. PARTY.

Being wheeled into St. Vincent's I've never been more relaxed. At ease and sedate. Rolling past nurses, orderlies and doctors, I eavesdrop.

Did you see Amoeban Idol last night...
They should trade him, salary or not...
I love the new smoking law...
Yeah, the concert was great, I really think it's going to make a difference. Like, everyone there was so unified, really. Bozo's speech was really touching...

Rolling on, I peep Lousifer. Pinned and focused.

Shit girl, I'm taking the long weekend. Ya feel me...
There was this guy last week, he had gangrene from shooting in his penis. Really interesting...
She didn't even know she had the hep...
And to think he lost his dad in 9/11...

Halting, we are curtained in. Lousifer and I.

'Yo Lous, let's get the fuck outta here.'

'No doubt.'

Lousifer peers around the curtain like a pedophile in a retirement home. 'Lay back and act normal.'

Sure thing, Lous.

I'm not sure if he's so sorted he fancies himself a doctor, but he calmly unlocks the wheels and pushes me to a handicapped bathroom, greeting his co-workers along the way...*hello doctor...good morning doctor...*

Breaching the stall, we rip all the needles, plugs, chords—lifelines—from my veins and make a run for safety. Surfacing on Seventh Avenue the sunlight is blinding, hypnotic.

Blood leaks from my veins, fills my eyes, mouth.

Shirtless and bleeding, I feel impervious to the winter. *Fuck it.* I don't even want a cab, I'll walk home. Fuck everyone.

Lousifer meets my eyes, gives a pound, hops a cab. I stroll down Seventh Ave.

It's five degrees, pre wind-chill. I have no idea the day, month, year, ruling party, latest pop monstrosity. Religion. Passing Bank, Perry, Charles, I leave a trail of blood. Islanders avert their eyes, speak on mobiles, send texts, place bets, order grams. I'm thirsty.

Reaching Bleecker I turn left, pass terrible tavern after trite watering hole until I come upon The Elongated Donkey Bar and Grill.

'Sir, we can't service you without a shirt.'

'Son, I'm Cracula. Give me a goddamn pint.'

Drinking and bleeding, I finally have time to think. *What now?* Dulces's a wrap. Slutskia still shares my residence. The Reverend's coming any day. I could go home, listen to The Fireman talk about his good friends. Listen to Aeronymous speak of The Cult. Listen to sames in predictive text. No, I shall become an astronaut. Experience weightlessness. Travel to Mars. I shall say things like 'Abort Mission' and 'Houston, Relax.'

Another pint please.

I'll travel the world, have a same in every country. Reproduce.
I'll befriend new Firemen, new clergy, urban wildebeests, sames,
unshaven decrees, shaven yields. Avoid cults. Having seen the
world, I shall have shrunk it. Then I'll be off to Mars, start a
new civilization. A new breed.

Check please.

Thirteen

The next few nights pass without incident. I avoid phone calls, watch sindemand, and pound whiskey. Aeronymous sends cult texts, The Fireman uses sames as steps, Tambourine is there in thpirit, Slave offers a reach around. Noddy understands. Lousifer begins dating Dulce. Slutskia can't figure out why I was carried out of our apartment. The Reverend arrives.

The Reverend's arrival, though welcome, will no doubt expedite the brewing shitstorm.

'Cracula, how are you man?'

Now, once again, a man of God. The Reverend speaks in thoughtful, measured tones. Atonal tones.

I offer him a drink, smoke.

'Cracula, I told you I quit smoking. Two years now.'

Resisting the urge to offer him a trophy, I pour two glasses of Malbec.

'Cheers.'

Indeed.

We sit, drink. I smoke reds. He speaks of Africa, the beauty, the struggles. I let him preach for hours. The Reverend lectures on Benin, Monrovia, Charles Taylor, Voodoo, slave trade, the Liberian constitution, Goodyear, lack of clean water, killing fields, landmines, cataracts, tumors (tumors!), bushrat, AIDS, old leaders, new leaders, UN policies, globalization. ETC.

'That's great Reverend, but how were the women? Surely there were some smoking villagers.'

'Cracula, I'm a changed man. I've taken an oath of celibacy.'

Come again. Cómo? Perdón? No! Dime la verdad. WHAT!?

He justifies and rationalizes longer than necessary, quoting scripture and that sort of thing. The Reverend finishes his rant by reminding me that homosexuality is a sin, though no worse than any other sin (?). Rendered retort-less, I open a fourth bottle of red and mention how much I enjoy his emails.

'Did you? I put a lot into them.'

He goes on to tell me how on some lonely nights he would mount his PC, sip wine, and picture himself a combination of Hemingway, Indiana Jones, and Robin Hood.

'Really? I can almost see it.'

He inquires on the status of The Fireman, Flow, Nowe, Tambourine, So, Dark—asks me if I've seen his ex-same Shia around.

'No one's changed Reverend.'

And how's my new same same, this Slutskia.

'She's the same Reverend. She'll be back in a few days.'

I open another bottle and he tells me he's had enough. This from a man that once could drink me under the table! Of course that was pre-oath. I show him his room, his sleeping quarters, and feel something bubbling under his sleeve.

'Cracula, are you around tomorrow?'

Sure Reverend, I'm around tomorrow.

At some point, I shut my eyes.

estaba soñando

I was inside one of the Cult meeting rooms on 1st and 1st— Kidding Now they called it. Only it was a yoga studio and the whole gang was there. Apparently we had all agreed to an hour of meditation. Nine mats lay on the ground—three by three. A seating chart hung on the wall.

Slutskia	*Fireman*	*Tambourine*
Aeronymous	*Cracula*	*Reverend*
Slave	*Lousifer*	*Dulce*

The Fireman was outfitted accordingly—regulation FDI boots, FDI pants—though he wore no shirt and reflexively flexed his oversized pecs. Sitting front and center, his palms faced up, rested on his knees. He pondered the possibility of the other eight spotting a gray hair he overlooked. *Had he tanned today?* He thanked his metro stars he hadn't eaten that bowl of rigatoni.

Tambourine was to The Fireman's right, she effortlessly assumed the lotus position. After all, she was thpiritual these days. In fact, at this moment she legally decided to change her name to Thpirit. She wore bright orange Buddhist monk attire, the first female to do so. Her right breast hanging free.

Slutskia made out the row on the left. The Cracula tattoo had crawled up her back, leaving a serpent's tail in its wake. The serpent spread, enveloping the poor girl, leaving her only human feature pasty, Russian, carpel-tunneled hands near her tail. Cracula resting between her eyes.

Behind Serpentskia was Aeronymous. He was Japanese—a Sumo! His tire-black hair was braided, splitting the enormity of his back. He was sans tats, save for BAPE across his forehead.

Staring at the back of Tambourine's head was The Reverend. He took the form of Jesus of Nazareth. Jesus donned in a Supreme Court robe. He stroked his beard.

Behind Jesus stood Dulce. Though when she looked down her mat was gone, replaced by Patpong road. Dulce was a Lady-Boy, virtually unchanged, save Adam's apple growth.

Left of the Adam's apple sat a samurai Lousifer, protected by red armor. Samurai sword slung over his back, face battle-ready.

To the warrior's left was Slave Carsons. He wore a blonde wig—Slutskia blonde—his face done up like a geisha. Above his pink g-string was a Cracula tattoo. He had a belly shirt on that read SON.

I flashed like a cursor in the middle, alternating
vampire
blood bank
vampire
blood bank

Johnny Cash walked in the room, he was to lead the meditation.

'Good afternoon Ladies, Gentlemen, Serpents, Lady-Boys, Vampires, Jesus.'

Baritone baby. Cash! *El hombre.*

'Let's hang our heads and pray. Heavenly Father, we are
gathered here today to elevate the minds of these fine creatures
of yours. Lord, help me that I might guide them to a warm place,
a clear place, a place that will show their heart's true desires
Lord. We pray that they may see the path ahead of them, that
they may take that knowledge Lord, and do with it what they
will. Thank you Lord. Amen.'

Johnny.

'Creatures of God, close your eyes with me now.'

All obliged, save Fireman staring at my lover's scales. *Cabron*.

'Open your souls God's children, open wider. Allow the Lord to
shine a light upon them. Now leave the shell of your physical
bodies behind. Float away and rise, rise God's children. Rise
above the mountains, rise above the sea, rise just below the
clouds, for you need to see. Below you are all the earth's oceans.
Keep your eyes closed and release your souls onto the water.'

The Fireman began a free fall, a nosedive. Leaving the comforts
of Cash's cloud he picked up velocity as he closed in on the sea.
FDI pants vanished, he was speedoed out as he made a Louganis-
perfect entry. He carried on, downward. He found himself in
the depths of the ocean.

The Fireman got head from a blowfish and took a gander.
Taking in the sharks, stingrays, plankton, clams, giant squids,
dolphins, crabs, and sperm whales, he vowed to become the
biggest fish in the sea. If he were to massacre the ecosystem in
the process, so be it. So he huffed and he puffed. An epic wind
tossed, tsunamis were birthed, continents shifted. The Fireman
turned Typhoon. He grew and grew until he broke the ocean's
surface. Razor in hand, he began to make calls.

'Hey Cracula, what's up? Hey, hold on that's my good friend Lark.'

'Hey Lark, hold on that's my good friend Daft.'

'Hey Daft, hold on that's my good friend Aria.'

The typhoon gained steam and added arms—a third, a fourth— each with razors.

'Hey Aria, hold on that's my good friend He.'

Fifth arm, sixth arm.

'Hey He, hold on that's my good friend Hymn.'

'Hey Hymn, hold on that's my good friend Spill Rates.'

The Fireman had a million arms—tentacles. A million razors.

The typhoon was a hurricane, the eastern seaboard ravaged.

'Hey Spill, hold on that's my good friend The President.'

Category ∞.

'Hey Mr. President, hold on that's my good friend Sharon.'

'Hey Ariel, hold on that's my good friend Mahatma.'

Typhoons were birthed in the Dead Sea, North Sea, China Sea, Pacific.

'Hey Gandhi, hold on that's my good friend Martin.'

Birmingham burned.

'Hey King, hold on that's my good friend Pol.'

Cambodia wept.

'Hey Mr. Pot hold on that's my good friend Abe.'

'Hey Mr. President, hold on that's my good friend Taylor.'

Gunshots rang out in Monrovia.

'Hey Chuck, hold on that's my good friend God.'

The earth's oceans boiled.

'Hey God, hold on that's my good friend Fred.'

'Hey man, thanks for the deal. My soul? You got it.'

I remained on hold.

Tambourine—*Thpirit*—remained in the clouds. She'd no desire to leave, ever. Already renamed, she decided to *be* thpirit. Thpirit in action. Combative, passive. Fuck the ocean, she floated upwards.

Blinded by the Sun, she breaststroked though the atmosphere, past the moon. Saturn, Uranus, Neptune in her rear view, she replaced Pluto. Thpirit was resolute in her evolution—she'd no idea it was a revolution.

Pluto downgraded, Thpirit upgraded.

Content on the outskirts of our system, far from the heat, Thpirit was our star's most distant satellite. She now needed a satellite of her own—a moon. Thpirit being Tambourine, her moon would no doubt be a homoerotic looking fellow named Bill, Bob, or Joe.

Viola! Thpirit settled into her rightful place outside Neptune, where she had not one, but three moons. Bill, Bob, and Joe looked on crescently.

There was no light, no water, no fire. *no life* Thpirit was content. She had her moons, and she was far from the stars.

Serpentskia slithered through the air, her stunted paws picking at her slimy scales. perusing the sea

'Bastaaaard!'

She skipped the waves and headed for an island. Crawling on the beach she sprouted arms, legs, breasts, an asshole. She was Slutskia again, save for the serpent's tail swinging from Cracula. She rose, walked on, tail dragging in the sand.

Slutskia came upon a single chair. As she took a seat, a mermaid swam to shore. Fins and gills melting into the sand, the mermaid put down a table and umbrella.

'What can I get you?'

'What u have?'

'We have a special today. Free pints of Cracula blood.'

'OK.'

Sipping my blood and wagging her tail, she caught wind of the ocean. Men rose from the waters, Greek men, Roman soldiers, Goliath, cabana boys, John Wayne. They were to feed her grapes, go down on her.

She wagged her tail.

The palm tree to her left became a woman—a goddess. Flowing Lao hair, Mexican skin, Dionysus limbs. The beach was no longer tree-lined, it was adorned with goddesses. Slutskia had her heirum.

She wagged her tail and ordered another round.

The Reverend—Jesus the Justice—accepted the ocean, its vastness, possibility. Its oath. After taking a moment to soak it in, he snapped his fingers and was standing on the sea. he walked for a bit

He walked the world over. Walked on water. Walked to the Supreme Court.

Already dressed the part, a gavel popped into his hand. He assumed his throne on the ocean. A panel of one. The world was non-existent, continents had yet to drift, no creatures crawled, no man, no apples. The Reverend was confounded. *Had his God sent him to purgatory?* He prayed, spoke to his God. He read the Bible, quoted passages. he screamed!

'Lord, why have you forsaken me?'

Left without anyone to judge, he banged his gavel.

Aeronymous the sumo floated below the clouds. Meditation or
not, he was far too dense to fool gravity and fell towards earth
like a bloated meteorite. Approaching a stormy sea, braided hair
pulled up, he said

FUCK IT SON

pulled knees to chest and unleashed the biggest cannonball since
the Civil War. Striking the ocean's bottom plates shifted, fault
lines rethought themselves. Aeronymous bounced off the earth's
core, aborting a calm sea. birthing a tidal wave.

He surfaced with the swell, afroed, and tan as a Ken doll. Neil
Young played from the heavens.

Surfing the grandest wave ever made, life's pressures were left
below with his previous girth.

The wave gained momentum and strength, as did Aeronymous.
No longer confined to The Cult, he guzzled Corona, did shots of
Patrón, and slammed every same he desired.

Dulce the Lady-Boy strolled along a cloud-laden Patpong road,
the night's conclusions endless. Fuck the ocean, she preferred
the dirt.

Not satisfied with the ex-pat options she plunged to the sea.
Escaping the Atlantic, Indian, Arctic, Pacific—she ended up in
the Gulf of Gack. Drowning in it, she backstroked to shore.

Once ashore, armies approached. cavalries, regiments, platoons,
divisions, brigades, navy seals, rangers, sharpshooters, snipers,
battalions. Che Guevara. The 3rd Reich.

She was on Omaha beach.
Ready to satisfy all comers.
Two by two, into the Ark.

The white sand was consumable, and she did.
line by line
soldier by soldier.

Lousifer the red samurai rode his white horse below the clouds

Glancing down, he witnessed the largest congregation of soldiers ever assembled. *Though no fighting took place?* They appeared to be in a line of sorts. two by two

He galloped towards the front, passing Alexander's army, Achilles, Hector, Napoleon, Heinrich, Santa Anna, Davey Crocket, Grant, Ike, Sitting Bull, Stallone.

he eventually arrived at the commotion's derivation

Dismounting, he presented his samurai sword and took on the world's army, slaying the most bloodthirsty soldiers. two at a time. Pinochet, Saddam, Nuan Chea, Sixtus IV, Ferdinand and Isabella, Rumsfield...

in the wake of blood and bodies, he beheaded and dismembered Dulce

Galloping away guilt enveloped him. *Goddamn it.* He returned to the recently beheaded.

'I'm sorry baby.'

'Me too.'

Slave skipped the clouds and headed to his home on CONSPIRE island

He'd undergone a sex-change operation. Gone to Argentina for tits, Thailand for a cunt. Grown flowing blonde locks and become a Reiki healer. Alone, he disrobed. Roamed Conspire Island.

Where art thou Cracula

Pained and alone, confusion set in. Had he not done everything possible to become my bitch. *Mi puta*.

did he regret getting CRACULA tattooed above his ass? did the galaxy not know his true desire?

Night fell. He looked skyward. Big Dipper, Little Dipper, Orion, North Star, Sirius, Canopus, Vega, Pollux. Spica.

Slave stared so long he saw me in the stars, spread his legs and masturbated

Wings spread, I flew through the clouds. Sorry Johnny, I don't feel like projecting my soul just yet.

i flew with the wind, against the wind, had a beer in a clear cloud, shut dope in a thunder cloud, downed a bottle of tequila in a funnel cloud and pissed in the ocean.

i checked into a guesthouse in the billows and stayed for what seemed an eternity, not a care in the world. no clue how long i was there, being timeless and all

Bored, I spread my wings and pterodactyled below the fog, gliding over the blue-eyed sea. Hank was wrong, it is beautiful.

i cruised the ocean in perpetuity, the wind's only sail

Tired of fresh air, I pierced the surface. wings replaced by a fin. teeth sharpened, gills formed. I had to keep moving.

Passing the mantle, I was at the core. The center of the world.

Cracula again. my fangs awoke, eyes darkened. resolve emboldened.

I found myself in a heptagon, a screening room of sorts. I sat in the middle below a projector, next to a telescope. The projector played in concert, snapping the screens to life.

a million-times-tentacled Fireman was expanding, slashing the world...a serpent-tailed Slutskia devoured her heirum and ordered another round...The Reverend inexplicably banged a gavel in thin air...Dulce lay beheaded, limbless, and Adam-appled...a samurai Lousifer galloped on the beach in remorseful triumph...Aeronymous surfed the big wave next to Crazy Horse...Slave played with his new vagina. through the telescope i spotted an icy Tambourine.

I was handed a control panel. *What was I to do with this?* I put it down, drank my wine, and crushed up an eightball.

Fourteen

Coming to, I am not alone. It appears a jury of sorts has been summoned. Descending my steps I enter the courtroom, the honorable Fireman presiding.

'Listen brother, we're all here to voice a joint concern we have.'

Is that right?

'Cracula?'

Yes Tambourine.

'You're lacking love and thpirituality in your life. Since we broke up years ago I've taken a thpiritual path, and it's lead me to love and understanding. So much love. Just look at my path, have I ever failed to get together with one of my boyfriend's friends after a break up? I never have, that's what thpirituality is all about. You need to keep the love close.'

At this point Tambourine reduces herself to some godawful pose and lets rip a deafening noise, a chant of sorts, from her belly.

'Ahmmmmm…my thpiritual advisor taught me this…ahmmmmmmmm….'

The Reverend speaks over the chant.

'Cracula, you've really let yourself go to shit. Writing my *Notes from West Africa: An Altruist's Journey*, I had no idea how far you'd fallen. Last night I prayed for you. Now, I don't know the answer, but you've got try another path. The Lord's path works for me.'

'Ahmmmmmmm……..'

'Yo Cracula!'

Yes Flow.

'You want a joint?'

'Not now Flow.' 'No!' 'Come on Flow.'

'Ahmmmmmmm………'

I pour myself a whiskey.

'Ahmmmmmmmmmmmmmm.'

'Cracula, what's up bro?'

Noddy?

'Listen maaaaan, I'm only here because….because…'

Noddy nods off, burning a hole in my couch.

'Listen Cracula, we all love you.'

Thanks Aeronymous.

'You need to give The Cult a try, it's done wonders for me.'

I can see.

'Ahmmmmmmmm……..'

The self-appointed foreman continues.

'We've found a place, a Cult Camp, in Rinsurvainsya.'

Oh have you?

'The Reverend and I have secured you a scholarship, so there will be no cost. Listen brother, when you come back you can be just like me. Don't worry about Slutskia, I'll keep an eye on her while you're gone.

'Ahmmmmmmmmmmm...'

The verdict rendered, Cult Camp it is.

Fifteen

I'm to depart for Rinsurvainsya—Cult Camp—in a week. But not before I keep to my prior plan of hitting London.

I pack for JFK and leave Slutskia a note.

Dearest Slutskia,

I'm off to London for a week of boozing, cavorting and overindulging. Upon my return, I shall be serving a sentence at a Cult Camp in Rinsurvainsya. There's vodka in the freezer.

Love,
Cracula

I call Delancey. Head to JFK.

'What carrier sir?'

'Amoeban Airlines.'

Entering Terminal C, I spot Borninne.

'Ohhhhmygod, what are you doing here?'

Catching a bus.

'Ohhhhmygod, where are you going?'

London.

'Ohhhhmygod, me too. Are you flying Amoeban?'

I am.

'Ohhhhmygod, do you want me to bump you to first class?'

No, I prefer a tight fit. 'Yeah, that would be lovely.'

Borninne has all the charming aspects of a trust fund same —
speaks French, flies first class, multiple homes, chooses her
friends, has a wine collection. She also has the inevitable
aspects — idle time to assign people *terrible* or *horrible,* drive her
boyfriend mad.

Latching onto Borninne's noble status, I pass the peasants
waiting on line and head to the Amoeban Elite counter.

'Yes, I'd like to use miles to bump up my friend.'

'Certainly, may I see your passport sir?'

Handing over my passport I approach one of those moments that
only occur when the rich and poor cross paths.

'OK sir, you're all set. I just need a credit card for the $400 fee.'

As class differences go, international flight is up there with The
Victorian Age. Nevertheless, handing over the Commerce debit
for $400 will slice 25% off my net worth.

'Here you go.'

What choice had I? Sit in economy? Grimace at the $400, forcing Borninne to pay it and relegate myself to son status? *Lo que sea.* I need a drink.

Waiting for X-rays and metal detection, Borninne informs me who is currently *awful* or *terrible*. The list is long.

Removing my belt, necklace, bracelet, shoes, keys, mobile, and loose change, I prepare to be molested.

'Sir can you step over here?'

Sure.

'Raise your arms. Sir, where are you headed?'

London.

'What is your purpose in London?'

None.

'Where are you staying in London?'

Not sure.

'How long are you staying in London?'

We'll see.

'With whom are you staying in London?'

Some dirty bird named Lurid.

I pound Hoegaarden at the bar and listen to Borninne. She speaks of plans, schedules.

'...then we're going off the coast of X, then we're taking a charter to Y, then we're meeting up with Z...'

First class means boarding first and drinking first—reckon I got a $400 open bar. 'Your finest bottle of red please.' They look at me though I'm afflicted.

We speak in Spanish, Borninne making fun of my Mexican accent. She teaches me grammar, manners. I watch in-flight Hollywood. Pass out to some nostalgic masturbation, *Hardened State*.

Sixteen

I never cease being awed when some foreign land allows me entrance.

The Brits must have paranoia-sniffing dogs, last time here I was strip-searched exiting the Chunnel. So it is with great shock that I enter the royal gates unscathed.

Borninne and I flee Heathrow and go our separate ways. She mounts her waiting Rolls, I queue up for a cab.

'Gackney please.'

Closing in on Gackney I send Lurid a text.

You up?

Quick response.

Still

Pulling up in front of her duplex, I spot Lurid passed out on the stoop. Forty in hand.

Lurid. Lurid, wake up. Yo...Lurid. I light a red and take a swig of her beer. Signs of life.

'Cracula! Baby, how arrre you?'

Hugs all around. We head for the local pub and proceed to chug vodka, do lines, smoke indoors.

Lurid's father was the guitar player in the best punk band of all time, Lurid is in a band, Lurid's boyfriend is in a band, Lurid's flatmates are in bands, Lurid's neighbors are all in bands, the boys Lurid cheats on her boyfriend with are in bands, Lurid's cousins are in bands, Lurid's heroes are in bands, Lurid's enemies are in bands, Lurid speaks of nothing but the latest band.

Despite this singularity, she can be loads of fun. During a session years back, she insisted on slicing me open and lapping up my blood. I still have the scars. Lurid can also be a drag.

In a blurred existence the following week is top ten. I summon all powers of detachment to avoid the reality of my upcoming sentence.

We go to gigs. We discuss gigs. We score gear. We rate gear. We drink, smoke, score, van, gig. Detach.

Leaving Lurid on her stoop, I head for Heathrow, JFK, The Island. Rinsurvainsya. Cult Camp.

Seventeen

I can't recall much of the drive to Rinsurvainsya. Just The Reverend speaking of divine intervention, free will, sin—some other nonsense. I remember praying for him to get some ass, at least a blowjob.

Reaching Cult Camp, dumped really, I find myself quarantined.

To be quarantined in a nut house is a goddamn achievement. I'm to be probed, prodded, investigated, drained of blood, urine—but not before induced sleep.

After a Cult nurse slams Cult narcotics in my veins, I'm led to a holding cell. An older Cult member enters, assuming ownership of my bags, clothes, me.

Post strip-search and molestation he starts on my backpack. The bastard removes the Amoeban first class bottles of Jack, Grey Goose, Patrón.

'You won't be needing these.'

Is red wine ok?

He, Cult member, moves on to my clothing. Confiscating the Singha beer t-shirt as evidence, same with the naked lady trailer trash tee.

'Might you please explain kind sir, why the problem with a scantily clad silhouette?

He, Cult member, adopts a stance so paternalistic oxygen excuses itself. I explain that in fact I'm the trash, the shirt making fun of me. A satire. He mumbles something about me being lost, seizes my wallet, crackberry, passport, iPod. Content with his molestation, he evacuates the cell.

As the cell door locks, The Cult narcotics begin taking effect. *I wonder if my entire sentence is to be carried out under such sedation?* That would be lovely. As I'm drifting off to a land of giant smurfs, flying dolphins, and Iggy Pop, the cell door flies open.

Forcibly escorted in is the most colossal bastard I've ever seen— 6'8", 300 pounds, 320 maybe. I'm informed Colossus scored a *.71* on the breathalyzer, a record. Offering congratulations I fear for my life. *Am I to meet my doom at the enormous paws of some drunk?* In Cult Camp! Fuck I need a drink.

Fortunately, after his molestation he collapses onto—and off of—his bed. *Que día!*

estaba soñando

I was in a castle, seeking escape. I climbed corridors, twisting
stairwells, roamed grand halls, indulged libraries, drank vino.
Pulled on door after door—all sealed. i was alone I screamed
to the gypsies below for help, rescue. They looked up and
smiled. scoffed. The sun would set soon, the dark powers
unleashed.

Retreating to my room, I locked the door and prayed. grasped
the bars on my window and watched the sun set over the
mountains. *fuck* My candle went out. freezing, sweating.
Waiting for the voices.

the shrieking whispers commence

At first they rolled in from the distance, inaudible had I not been
in a trance. Hypnotized. my blood thickens, richens. The room
exhaled spiders, flies, serpents. The roaring whisper gained
steam through the mountains. Wolves. Gypsies.

Back against a stone wall, the whisper entered my quarters,
impregnating the shadows with demons, vamps. My jugular
pulsateed, pounded, on the verge of implosion. The shadows
brandished knives, fangs, and whispered my name.

Harker...Harker

Eighteen

'Cracula, wake up. You're to see the psychiatrist now.'

I'm led to the shrink's office by a young Cultesse. Her hips seem to widen as we walk. She munches a candy bar, chugs Coca-Cola, and wonders aloud when she'll have time for a smoke break.

'Wait here sir.'

OK.

'Cracula, the doctor will see you now.'

OK.

'Cracula, I'm Dr. Cult.'

I see.

'I'm going to ask you a few questions. I just want to get an idea of where you're at.'

Serving a sentence in Rinsurvainsya Doc.

'Do you ever have homicidal thoughts?'

Sure, I live in The Island.

'Do you ever have suicidal thoughts?'

Only when feeling down.

'Cracula, do you have a grasp on what's real and what isn't?'

Only when dreaming.

'Do you hear voices? Hallucinate?'

Whenever possible.

'Do you have a healthy relationship with the opposite sex?'

Define sex.

'Do you have a healthy infrastructure of friends, people you can rely on?'

Can you repeat the question? Define the word friend? Give the Latin derivation?

Returning from her smoke break, the Cultesse leads me back to my holding cell, fresh candy bar in hand. I stare at the sleeping behemoth as the door locks behind me. I've no books, no music, no sindemand. No escape.

The Cult nurse enters my cell, slams me with Cult narcotics. Tells me happy Valentine's Day.

I mimic the giant's breath until I pass out.

estaba soñando

I'd been given a job at Ballmark. My first assignment was to design this year's Valentine's Day card and ad campaign. I submitted the following.

This Valentine's Day say it with baking soda

<u>Donkey</u> (dông-ke) n. pl. keys
    1. The domesticated ass.
    2. An obstinate or stupid person.

I deplore couples

There is not a single thing that strains my blues more than two
Islanders that have taken it upon themselves to form a couple
Are they not superfluous enough alone?
Must they spread their insidious hole?

More eclipsing than a couple?
A couple holding hands
Worse yet?
A couple holding hands in the park, juxtaposing their tragedy
amongst the trees, grass, innocent dogs.

Shall I continue? I shall
A couple walking on the beach, molesting my view.
Sipping wine. Sipping !
Discussing the world of pop. Planning. Feigning.

Worse yet?
Those souls that ponder nothing but the abysmal day that they
too will be a couple.
Must they proliferate? They must.

Most moronic of all?

Bastards fortunate enough to be emancipated, yet blinded by the rearview mirror.

This Valentine's Day, scream it loud,
I'm wacked and I'm proud.

At this point Tambourine entered the dream. She told me I was alone and needed thpirituality in my life. The same would not get off on sarcasm if it went down on her.

Nineteen

'Cracula, come with me please.'

The Cultesse has graduated to a Klondike bar, three-liter root beer.

'You're to see Dr. Feelgood now. He'll tell you the blood test results and do a medical intake.'

Is there a difference?

'Cracula!?'

Yes Dr. Feelgood.

'Come in my office!'

Sure.

'Shut the door behind you!'

When driving, I've always been paranoid of a trailing police car. I'm dumbfounded when a foreign land stamps my passport. I'm flat-out dismayed when helicopters don't land in my living room. BLOOD TEST RESULTS?

'Cracula, are you a fan of irony?'

I guess it depends.

'Well I am. That's why I've legally changed my name to Dr. Feelgood. Do you think people leave here feeling good? Feeling better than before they came?'

The world is full of masochists.

'Cracula, I can see I'm not reaching you. You're one of those Islander bastards. You think you're above The Cult, better than The Cult. You actually believe you don't need The Cult. I'm here to tell you that if you don't accept The Cult into your life YOU ARE GOING TO DIE!

Now, I have your blood test results, *your full blood test results*, right here. But we'll get to that shortly. First, let's do a quick medical intake. Cracula, do you exercise?'

I live in a third floor walk up.

'How many cigarettes do you smoke daily?'

Depends on how much yack I've done.

'How much cocaine do you consume daily?'

Depends on how much I've had to drink.

'How much do you drink daily?'

That's a loaded question. It depends on my current latitude, longitude, same same situation, political climate, last book I've read, days since my last heroin overdose, proximity to inventors, financial situation, level of exposure to bad Hip Hop. Have I been forced to watch Hollywood?

'Cracula, I don't like you.'

Terribly sorry.

'Let's move on to the results from your blood work.'

Please God. Please! I will go to church. I will call my mom, volunteer in Africa, speak the truth. Write in the third person.

'Cracula.'

Yes doc.

'It troubles me deeply to inform you that despite your sexual misconduct, illicit drug use, alcohol abuse, chain smoking, and overall freewheeling approach to life…you're healthy as a virgin triathlete.'

Goddamn that was close.

'Don't make the mistake of thinking this will last young man. Your time will come. Now get out of my office!'

Returning to my cell, I'm so giddy I can almost forgive the Cultesse her gallon of rocky road.

Twenty

Eventually I'm admitted to the general population. My
roommate is some gay fellow named Audit. By far the gayest
gay man I've come across. Gay with life, gay with being in Cult
Camp, gay with working for the DIE RS, gay with being gay.
Every so often he forgets to flush, leaving me a gay log. I don't
care, he does my laundry.

There are quack shacks and there are...Cult Camps. They assign
insane persons a schedule, a to-do list. *They rate your bed-
making ability.* If the world is an asylum, The Island is its loony
bin, Cult Camp its recycle bin.

I am subjected to schedules, feelings—eating breakfast! And
what do we do post-cereal? We nutcases break into groups of
public defenders, jurors, defendants—all the while judge and
prosecutor.

And how did that make you feel...
What were the repercussions of that action...
How was your partner affected...
*What do you think the long term effects on your children will
be...*
What would God do...

feelings. repercussions. partner. long term. children. god.

Are they mad?

Most disturbing is my fellow prisoners' eagerness to partake—
role play. Only their innate ability to embellish keeps me
attentive.

'I guess it all started with my first boyfriend. Well not really my boyfriend, more like my stepmom's boyfriend…he just kept offering me pills, white wine, triple-X movies. I mean, like, I was only 10 and I was like sure. Then we just kept having sex. How did I feel? Well, I like, loved it.'

All the whackos feign gasps and wait their turn on stage. The proctoring Cultesse chimes in.

'Georgia, what part did you love?'

'You mean what part of the sex?'

More feigning.

'No. The alcohol, drugs, pills.'

'Well, like, I just figured I was home. Ya know…like I had gone home.'

At this point the Cultesse calls on the other inmates to comment on the southern belle's plight. The first is this horrible prick from Boston, Counter.

'Well Georgia, in essence it is a home you've always sought, and a home you still seek. The first avenue of a home that was introduced to you, by this horrible gentleman I might add, gave a temporary sense of relief, a home if you will. Since then your entire life has been spent seeking this home, this refuge.'

We, the jurors, sit silently as the retarded mongrel of a judge renders our defendant her verdict. Meanwhile, he's four days off meth.

'What you need to do is seek out a new home, a home without preying men, without mind-altering devils, you can find a home in The Cult. I have.'

The bastard sits back, basking in congratulatory eyes. Georgia paints on tears and drools over Counter like a candy cane. I seek flight. The Cultesse, our mediator, asserts herself.

'Georgia, how did Counter's elegant proclamation make you feel?'

'It made me feel, like…well, like I have love here.'

Satan, I need a gun.

'You do have love in The Cult. Georgia, would you like a hug?'

Georgia, relegating herself to teddy bear, laps it up.

My mind bounces through time and space. I am a Viking, a beer swigging Viking, only I live on Venus and sail oceans of fire. Off the bow is a village of young wenches, young and willing Venusian wenches. They scream…

'Cracula?'

Yes Cultesse.

'Would you like to give Georgia a hug?'

Mierda!

This is bad. Downright entrapment. *Would this knock time off my sentence?* Good behavior and all. What to do?

'Uh...Miss Cultesse...Proctresse...uh...I'm terribly sorry, but I'm physically unable to perform said act at this time.'

With my declaration Georgia surpasses tears and usurps convulsions. Audit springs to life and performs some sort of gay Heimlich maneuver, bringing the belle back to life. My fellow jurors turn prosecuting judge and cast firing-squad eyes on me. The proctresse intervenes.

'Cracula, what do you see as a downside to Cult living?'

'Well...the thought of never having an intravenous collision with a random comet of revelation careening toward one of my poles, sure to both handicap and heighten my galactic antennae's clarity...followed by eons of sucrose-coated conformity, handheld attrition, cerebral circumcision, premeditated mating, and a house in the flatlands? All the while daily force-fed three hot meals of Genericana for eternity? Go fuck yourself.'

Even in the land of loonies, there must be an outcast.

Twenty-One

The nights here are utter terror. *How is one to sleep unadulterated?* No wine, no comedown. The initial moons fill with regular visitors—demons, vampresses, Satan, white light.

I deduce, empirically of course, that the onset of terror is caused by my newfound and unnatural body chemistry. I alert The Cult leaders to my discovery, they are not sympathetic.

'Cracula, you know what your problem is?'

The reels play on.

'You refuse to live in reality. You actually *choose* to live in the clouds.'

Does one choose his place of birth?

'Cracula, you just need to take things as they are. You need acceptance. You need to accept The Cult.'

Accepting my quandary, I retreat to my room. Prepare for a night of visitors.

estaba soñando

I was in Cult Camp, in bed. Only with no roommate and strapped in. The concrete walls replaced by bamboo. I could hear a not so distant ocean, calm waves.

I summoned all my loony strength, tried to break free, no dice. These cult bastards could really tie a knot. I suppose this was The Cult way of forcing acceptance.

accepting my demise, i shut my eyes. tried to sleep

On the verge of dreaming, the bamboo began buzzing with life. At first the noise dispersed throughout the wall and ceiling, then purposefully converged in the wooded support beam near my head. My strapped-in head!

Rolling my eyes to the left, I tried to locate the resting place of the buzz. the wooden support beam began to bubble...It was as if the outside had been splashed with acid, prisoners inside seeking escape.

acid and inmates converged, producing one pulsating, impending bubble. Was this real? *have the cult bastards hypnotized me?*

The bubble made its way down the wooden support beam, coming to a rest inches from my face. The throbbing escalated, picked up speed. Calling for help was pointless. *The bastards are probably watching.* I accepted the terror, accepted my fate.

on the verge of resolution, the bubble actually made contact with my face. again and again. contact. recoil. eventually

Climax.

My face was blasted with sap. Layers of sweet, oozing sap.

Opening my eyes, I examined the hole that replaced the bubble.
The buzzing lessened—seemed to take a collective breath—only
to gain strength in the form of one singular roar. *What have
these cult bastards done?*

The roar turned growl, reverted to buzz, and dispersed amongst
thousands of flies hovering over the sap. *Hovering over my face.*
The flies broke into attack formation, picked up the volume, and
pounced on their midnight snack. Through the buzz—the
smorgasbord—I looked back to the hole. One by one, a gang of
spiders began making their way—jumping from the beam to my
bed, over my strapped-in shoulders. Hundreds of them marched
toward the flies. towards my face

rendered comatose, i accepted the spider onslaught, my fate
The Cult's Will

wanting to contribute to this newly formed ecosystem, i
consented to the spider bites. they feasted on the flies, on the
sap. on me.

'Cracula. Cracula, CRACULA!'

Hmm...

'Time for breakfast.'

Twenty-Two

Facing a day of Cult brainwashing, I'll need my strength. I hit the mess hall, order blueberry pancakes with extra syrup, eggs, bacon, ham, hash browns, and five decaf coffees.

Men and sames are separated during meals, it's The Cult way. Mess hall conversation never varies. *How did you receive your sentence...Where are you from...I did that too...*

This always digresses to the search for common ground—pop music, sports, Hollywood. Fucking torture. *How do these loonies talk of such things sans yack?* Or at least two bottles of red? The interjection of a novel is immediately thwarted by a self-help book or, god help us, a book on thpirituality. *Is anything on earth more of a fraud than non-fiction?*

Sober, I head to the butt hut—need to wash down the cholesterol and moronic banter with four or five reds. Holding court is the Frenchman.

Yann is the most well-read, traveled, over-educated fellow I've ever come across. A wino and cokehead. Speaks fifteen languages, taught at Oxford, was a UN diplomat, published ten books of philosophical critique, a leading French and English historian, composer and playwright. Blames the Jews for everything. To be in his company is to be stranded on a cruise with Voltaire's shadow.

Coughing, I head to a Cult lecture on physical health.

All the loonies file into The Cult auditorium—men on the left, sames on the right. And who is to lead the lecture on healthy living? None other than the ever-widening Cultesse that roams the halls of the holding cell.

Despite the loonies having taken their designated seats, the Cultesse is in no rush to finish her foot-long dog—cheese running down her cheeks. She sports a Rinsurvainsya State t-shirt that appears life-sized. Her spiel begins with the last bit of leftover cow, mustard, queso, relish, and onions still in her mouth.

'OK loonies…today…we…are …going to talk…about…'

The Cultesse falls silent, appears frozen. She reaches for her throat and begins throwing her head about like a possessed rottweiler. Not sure if this is a Cult healthy living technique to be followed later, the loonies watch silently and with full attention. A few of the sames go so far as imitating her flailing, standing in place and thrashing the air.

Amidst the confusion a 300-pound bearded Cult orderly barrels down the aisle and pounds on her back, only heightening the confusion. This causes some of the men to breach the aisle, pound sames' backs. Caught between the spectacle to my right and the Cultesse in front, I almost miss the projectiled remnants of the foot-long dog—cow bits, bun, queso, small children.

With order eventually restored, the Cultesse goes on preaching physical health as if nothing happened. Unable to control my laughter, I'm removed.

Twenty-Three

The endless cycle of eating, smoking, judging, being judged, laughing, and reaping nightmares carries on. After an unspecified number of sunsets, I'm permitted a phone call.

'Haaalo, who fauk this?'

'It's me.'

'Who fauk this.'

'Slutskia, it's me.'

'Who me?'

'Cracula, your boyfriend.'

'Baybee, where fauk u are?'

'Didn't you get the note? I'm in a Cult Camp in Rinsurvainsya.'

'Baybee, I see faukin note. U no I not read English.'

'Didn't The Reverend tell you?'

'Reverend go Africa. Baybee, what Cult Camp? Rinsvain? And where fauk is vodka?'

'Don't worry babe, I'll be home soon. The vodka's in the freezer. Everything OK?'

'No baybee, I faukin pregnin.'

Que?

'Baybee, you faukin hear me? I faukin pregnint.'

'Well that's great babe, I love kids. You sure?'

'Yes, I faukin sure baybee!'

'OK, OK. So listen, I'll be out of here soon, and I'll get back to work, start saving for our son, daughter. Maybe in the meantime you should take it easy on the vodka, maybe cut out the smokes.'

'Cracula, I not have faukin baybee.'

'What?'

'Baybee, how we have deees keed? We not haveeng money. You faukin drug addeeek.'

'Slutskia, why do you think I'm in Cult Camp?'

'Baybee, is no possible. I have give money my parents, my seeester. U not fadder.'

'Slutskia, let's talk about this when I come home. I'm sure we can figure it out.'

'Baybee, is not possible.'

'I'll be home soon, just take it easy until then. OK?'

'OK baybee. I lauv u.'

'Love you too.'

Hanging up the phone I'm high on life. The possibility of life. A new life. I feel my veins pump blood to my face, irrigating out irony. I'm not the least bit concerned about Slutskia's state of mind, no doubt I could rectify it. I vow to give in to The Cult, accept The Cult. After all, I'm to be a father.

Twenty-Four

The rest of my sentence is served nightmare-free. I wake on time, ready for the torturous breakfast conversation. I discuss pop music, football, gossip Hollywood. I role-play.

I, free and of my own will, accept my turns as judge, juror, prosecutor. When called on, I dole out hugs. At every opportunity I find common ground, I seek low common denominators—live The Fireman. I phone Aeronymous, letting him know I've accepted The Cult in my life. He's pleased. I'm pleased he's pleased. I please people daily. I'm pleased being a people pleaser. I even go to The Cult gym—body conscious. I phone Tambourine and chant thpiritual chants. I vow not to hold The Reverend's delusions against him.

As I've kept my impending fatherhood to myself, The Cult leaders are shocked and impressed at my abrupt turnaround. They hammer in me not to forget that The Cult is behind my newfound peace, and to cease living The Cult lifestyle would lead to my past dementia. I concur. Upon taking the oath of The Cult, I'm to be released tomorrow morning. But not before my last night's sleep at Cult Camp.

Lying in bed drunk with the morning's anticipation, Audit attempts a conversation of sorts.

'So Cracula, have you always been into sames?'

Oh lord, here we go. Fuck it, I'll play along. 'What precisely do you mean Audit?'

'Well, you know, if like everything was just perfect would you consider…'

At this point I have no idea how long my sentence has been, but I know I'm leaving tomorrow. That said, if one receives a blowjob in the forest with no one around, does it make a noise? This has been quite the period of abstinence. Maybe it would do some good? Ahh…but I'm a father to be, wouldn't want to ordain some cosmic common law.

'Yeah, I've always been into sames.'

estaba soñando

i was laying in bed with slutskia, only i was a SUPERHERO.
one centimeter tall. C.M. they called me   my only power was
walking through walls.

i found myself standing on the mole above her left boob, similar
to balancing atop a fire hydrant. my first obstacle, MOUNT
SAINT DUBBALDEE, directly in front of me. i was equipped
with a utility belt and phaser.

stepping off the hydrant, i slackened some rope from my belt,
attached a bowie knife to the end and harpooned SLUTSKIA'S
nipple.

as i began my ascent the sleeping LEVIATHAN tossed and
turned, leaving me hanging on for dear life. afraid she might
wake up, i set the phaser to stun and took aim.

tremors over, i carried on, the NIPPLES proving themselves
sufficient leverage for the smooth-skinned climb.

winded when i reached the summit, i took a smoke break, ate a
PowerBar. scratched my balls. quite a view, this female.
mountains, valleys, freckles, precarious fault lines, peninsulas,
dried-up river beds. would be a great place to eat some shrooms.
wonder if my guy delivers to dreams?

ahh…but i have a mission, gotta keep moving. i put out my
stoge, began the descent

repelling down the south face of DUBBALDEE the rope began
to fray, unraveling near the nipple. *fuck* i picked up the pace,
tried to avoid disaster.   too late   the rope snapped, hurling me
toward an impending RIB.

as fortune would have it, SLUTSKIA inhaled at the moment of impact, softening the blow. i escaped with a sprained ankle. catching my breath between ribs, my brain rattled with her heart's BEAT.

ready to embark on the second leg of the journey, my worst fears were realized

'BAYBEE, WHAT FAUK U DUU?! WHY THERE IS HARPUUN IN MY NIPPLE BAYBEE?! FAUK CRACULA! I TRY TUU SLEEP. U R BAASTAAARD...U...'

my phaser still on stun, i zapped her forehead. *lights out*   the coast now clear, i set out for my destination.

up and down i floated with the expansion of each breath. over ribs and greenland SKIN, stopping north of the grand innie. i smoked my last red, took a shot of wheatgrass, gargled Listerine, sanitized my hands.

then i invoked my super power

into SLUTSKIA i ventured   the belly of the beast   through her epidermis, dermis, subcutaneous tissue   past melanin, nerve endings, sweat glands, oil glands, hair follicles, blood vessels, pacinian corpuscles   hurdled the uterus   entered the WOMB
        suspended next to my lineage

swimming over, i looked for signs of gender

'what the hell are you doing here?'

guess it's a girl

'sorry sweetie, i'm your father.'

'oh i know, i've heard all about you. mom's always going off on some tangent, usually in Russian. by the way, would you mind telling her to chill on the smokes? it's getting pretty damn cloudy in here.'

'sure sweetie, anything else?'

'actually yeah. if she must drink vodka, tell her to stick to Grey Goose, straight up. all that sugar is fucking killing me.'

'hey, watch your mouth.'

'look who's talking pops.'

true

'and daddy?'

'yes dear?

'please give me a normal name. i don't know what the hell my grandparents were thinking. *cracula? slutskia?* are you fucking kidding me?'

'did you have anything in mind?'

'dad, i don't even know what's out there. i just don't want to get made fun of in school. anyway, aren't you supposed to be the creative one? just don't pigeonhole me before i'm even born. god!'

'ok sweetie, anything else?'

'don't paint my room pink, no daisy wallpaper, none of that shit. cool?'

'cool.'

'dad, i'd love to chat, but i'm supposed to have another seven months of peace and quiet. there will be plenty of time for all this get to know you shit. *comprende?*'

'*si* babe. give me a hug.'

'bye daddy, love you.'

'love you too, see you soon.'

Twenty-Five

'Cracula, someone is here for you.'

The Reverend's arrival means the end of Cult Camp, return to
The Island. A new way of living. I'm to be an assembly line
worker, an obtuse symbol in a formula. And why not? The
Island itself has become part of a formula, no longer its own.
Where blood once spotted the streets, money has taken over.
Money in the charade of business. People *doing* business.
Business as deconstruction. Business speaking business.
Business meetings. I fucking despise it ALL ITS
ENTITLEMENT AND PRECOCIOUSNESS.

The most vile spawning of all? *Business partners.* Is nothing
more doomed to implode? Even more than an Island marriage?
Partners? Masturbatory rowboats. Reliant on one another to go
upstream. At the first sign of taking on water it's every man for
himself.

It continues. The alluding to one's money via business, whom
you are in business with. *I've done some business there.* Indeed
it's who you are in bed with—waiting for the other to pass out so
he can get fucked first. Business is a form of invention even the
poor can play, must play.

What business are you in? ever so lightly bantered by sames.
The retort? Ranging from aphrodisiac to phallic conclusion.
Business has always dominated The Island. But now! It has
driven a stake through The Island's heart, exorcised its soul. A
tide independent of moon. No more art galleries, shooting
galleries, sucking galleries. Just a gang of posers filling up a
convention center. So why shouldn't I accept The Cult? In a
city that systematically assassinates free spirits every bastard
joins something.

'What's up Reverend?'

'Cracula, how are you man? You look great.'

Years ago, that would have no doubt been a piss taker. These days he's a man of God, and we're both men of oaths.

Should I share the news? If anyone is to be confided in, it's The Reverend. Reckon I would even take comfort in his Biblical assurances. Hmm…not yet.

'Reverend, I'm officially a Cult member.'

'Wanna grab a beer?'

Thank god he hasn't lost all sarcasm.

Jaunting the Rinsurvainsya hills, Slutskia—pregnant Slutskia—commandeers my head. All doomsday thoughts washed away by my Cult Camp experience. For now, I am dutiful, purposeful. *Am I a man of conviction?*

Driving on, the oh-so-well-meaning Reverend speaks in beautiful, colorful proclamations. Darwin personified—his latest evolution. The modern face of the Jesus world—the fittest. Though part of his evolution, his survival, is to deny IT. Most entertaining.

Well Cracula, the Bible says…Lewis says…Falwell says…

I bite my tongue.

He's painting quite the picture—long, shallow, played-out brushstrokes. Primary colors. *Do all of nature's venomous creatures not come in stunning, bright, blinding packages?* Life-ending snakes, frogs, fish, salesmen, politicians, berries, television.

You have so much to be thankful for. You can't imagine what I've seen in Africa...

I draw blood.

Is it already time to compare and contrast? Have we reached The Island already? Has The Reverend, my dear Reverend, already transformed to an Islander that lives there only to reap the spoils and crucify the inhabitants? A true businessman. An evolved businessman. The evolved business of God.

Most importantly Cracula, we must think of how our actions influence and affect our parents. Do you take them into consideration?

I sever my tongue.

Choke on it. Spew blood. *Parents!* Is nothing in the galaxy more of a cop-out? Seeking solace in mommy and daddy? Have not wars been fought, racism maintained, ignorance adhered to, gods worshipped, political parties joined—politics joined! Businessmen made. Parents: religion's stepson.

I shall teach my daughter everything I know, then have her burn it. Smoke it if she likes.

Nearing The Island life's variables race through my head. Fireman, Lousifer, Dulce, Noddy, Aeronymous, Tambourine, Slutskia, Slave, Hugatcha, Feather, So, Nowe, Flow, Lark, ladder dwellers, inventors, same sames. Satan, God.

My daughter.

I block out life's pleasantries—booze, crack, foreign sames—focus on The Cult.

Between measured breaths I meditate over my place in the formula. I shall make myself easily divisible, a square root. I shall start every conversation low. I'll address thpirituality, watch TV, masturbate to Hollywood. Discuss reality shows. I will fit in.

Entering the Fallen Tunnel, The Island's fallopian tube, I'm a single sperm cell. Emerging Island-side, I'm a fully developed Cult member.

We circle yuppies, pass Chinatown, and head north on Inventor Ave. Up Dead Broadway, Past Flipriani's, Wiesel, Sames On Posters. Turn right on Spring.

Climbing the steps behind 109 I feel fresh, alive. Like I never left the stretcher. My incubator awaits.

'Slutskia, I'm home.'

'Hey baybee.'

The first hug sends shockwaves, electric currents, humanity.

'Lauv u baybee.'

I love you.

It all seems real enough, timely in the least. Dropping to my knees, I press my head towards the future.

I'm revived, mistakenly given purpose.

'Baybee, what u duu?'

Looking after my daughter dear. Ahh...a family, the Amoeban dream. She shall travel the world, converse in multiple tongues. Know enough of politics to despise, possess her father's eyes. Only speak sardonically when needed. Be a native. My daughter shall do all these things. Or none.

'Baybee, I tell you I no have keed now. I cannot baybee. How you be fadder. U tuu crazy baybee.'

How do I explain The Cult to Slutskia? To my daughter's mother? Do my eyes not pronounce rebirth? Are they not the proper amount of blue, white, black. I'm sure after a few days without helicopters, conversing with imaginary people, or cutting myself...she'll come around.

'Babe, we'll talk about this later. I gotta meet up with the boys.'

'Baybee, you baastaaard!'

I leave Slutskia to a shower and walk over Spring and up Elizabeth to Café Uponya.

Aeronymous, Lousifer, and Noddy waiting. Aeronymous no doubt will be the first to greet, a customs greeting.

'Yo Cracula, what's up son? What's the deal? You look good man.' Leans in. 'Welcome to The Cult. Feel free to reach out to me at any hour regarding anything Cult. That's my word son, love you bro.'

Alas, I'm back in the land of words and sons. Downtown Island, son. *Palabra*

Aeronymous has done the impossible, the unthinkable, the unattainable. The man has enlarged! Not only is he girthier, he's acquired a BAPE sweater whose brightness transcends the color wheel. It simply glows. A ginormous, shipwrecked dinoflagellate.

'No doubt son.'

Lousifer's next.

'What up homey? You good, man? Missed you son.'

Lousifer informs me he joined The Cult the day I left, and has been living The Cult lifestyle the same amount of time as me. I feel looked up to, guilty.

Noddy gives a warm embrace, fresh cig burns on his jacket.

'Love you bro. You know my deal, but I got your back on this whole Cult thing.' Thanks Noddy. 'And if you ever step back to the dark side I got you there too.' Word.

We take our seats in Café Uponya, a table for five. I enjoy the chicken mole. Lousifer orders steak and fries. Noddy lights a stoge, passes out. Aeronymous speaks Cult and devours four cheese enchiladas, a chicken diablo sandwich, rice and beans, eight ears of corn, seven Jarritos, coconut flan.

We say our goodbyes, go our separate ways. Lousifer to collect, Noddy to get loaded and listen to Bite Eyes and Friona, Aeronymous to contort and binge on iced coffee (extra sugar). Me? Home to the wife and kid.

Twenty-Six

Verbally, the next few hours are a tug of war. I speak of The
Cult, the new Cracula. Slutskia speaks of helicopters and
parents. I propose a new day, she recalls our worst day. Future.
Past. My present. Her present.

Mentally, I'm adrift. I dream names and first words. Hair color.
How her eyes will stand against the ocean. Losing baby teeth.
Playing with puppies. Slutskia's view doesn't concern me, she'll
come around.

Tonight we're to join The Reverend for dinner at some new
Meatpacking outpost, Judas Bar. Apparently he's starting a
charity all his own and is seeking dinero. Ever the evolver.
Tonight's dinner is a reach-out(around) to potential donors. This
of course means a table full of inventors, businessmen, cunts,
good friends, and table-setting sames. Or for me, the first test of
The Cult's power.

Twenty-Seven

Slutskia, our seed, and I hop in Delancey, head west.

Judas Bar is a monster of an establishment, equipped with a 50-foot Judas statue in the center of the room.

'What party are you with sir?'

The Reverend.

'Right this way.'

Walking towards the circle-jerk an article I read the other day flashes in my head. *In Ducks, War of the Sexes Plays Out in the Evolution of Genitalia.* There's these ducks whose cocks go through a growth spurt every year leading up to mating season. These duck dicks sometimes wind up running the entire length of the duck, in the shape of a corkscrew. Literally spiral out of control. This in response to the female ducks' elongated, spiraling snatches. Apparently the duck with the longest schlong has first choice. The only catch is, after shooting a few spiral loads, the duck dick falls off! A detachable penis.

We have the largest table in the pond, in front of the statue. The Reverend sits at the head wearing an ill-fitting black suit. He's flanked by uptown do-gooders, inventors. The table continues with Flow and his same, Nowe and his same, Fireman and eleven Brazilian sames, Slave Carsons, Treimee, businessmen.

Due to our tardiness, the only two remaining seats are next to an inventor named Dickless Lament. We plug in and go through the requisite kiss-kiss, hugs, handshakes, pounds, nice to meet ya's. Everyone thrilled with my return. Amazed by my appearance. Dismayed by my eyes.

It's inevitable that Dickless Lament will comment on the food,
wine, same sames. And in the most WASPY stance imagined.
*This vino is acceptable. That said, have you been to The South
of Fraunce? HA HA. You've yet to encounter a more glorious
breed of nobles popping champagne. The amount of money I
spend is unimaginable to you. Really. HA HA. Have you ever
tasted a '72 Rothschild. HAH. I live '72 Rothschild in The
South of Fraunce. Did I mention South of Fraunce? HA HA.
South of Fraunce. Imagine the experience. HA HA. You should
come. I don't know if you could afford it though. HA HA.*

I wonder if he could afford his own funeral? I wonder if he
knows the taste of vomit in the morning. Does he know the view
from a K hole? Has he experienced Nurcan afterworld?
Speedball revolution? The born rich cunt! A night or five at St.
Vincent's? Fucking without daddy's help? Has he ever looked
in the mirror and been forced to see himself?

Do any of these bastards ever take on another's lens? Am I the
only man in The Island with bad eyes? I look at Dickless
Lament and pull out my shank.

*South of Fraunce. South of Fraunce. South of Fraunce. South of
Fraunce. South of Fraunce. South of Fraunce. South of Fraunce.
South of Fraunce. South of Fraunce. South of Fraunce. South
of...*

I shank his WASP eyes and ravage his WASP jugular. He poses
on...

*South of Fraunce. South of Fraunce. South of Fraunce. South of
Fraunce. South of Fraunce. South of Fraunce. South of Fraunce.*

Grabbing his WASP tongue I slice it off, put it on my spoon, pull the cotton from my ears, add water, boil, pull a point out of my jacket, bang my arm! I'm loaded on rich WASP cunt.

I've been on many trips—speedball island, yack moon, heroin bay, planet k, ganja reef, whiskey strait, mdma house, crystal beach, yabba-dabba-doo—this is my first born-rich WASP mainline. Dickless Lament running through my veins.

Filled with the soul of WASP cunt, my lenses flip, fangs retract, entitlement grows. I view my subjects.

I shall allude to my wealth, only specify when called for. I shall hover flippantly, pretend I did things. I shall offer travel. Offer *The South of Fraunce!* I shall never cheat. I shall have mistresses, epic affairs. I shall play polo and wear it. I won't travel The Island, I shall do the islands. I shall dine in Amoeba and propagate its ineptitude.

I shall look in my imported mirror and slit my throat.

Ahh...I will do none of these things. I will find common ground, apply formulas. I will fit in.

'Can I get you a drink?'

'I take vodka.' Could she not at least stick to wine?

'And for you sir?'

Diet Coke.

I tune out Dickless and watch The Fireman in action. His powers have increased...

'The owner of this place is a good friend of mine. He owns the Paris Judas Bar with another good friend of mine. Hold on that's my good friend calling from LA. 'HEY DON...NOT MUCH...JUST EATING AT JUDAS BAR WITH SOME GOOD FRIENDS...YEAH, I CAN DO THAT FOR YOU...SHE'S A GOOD FRIEND OF MINE...I'LL HAVE MY PEOPLE START ON IT.'

The sames are mesmerized, caught in a spell, tractor beamed. I Cultishly think how I might aid, plug in.

'Who was that, Fireman?'

'Oh, just my good friend in LA. You know Don, the richest guy in Lost Aimless.' Speaking to me, for the sames.

'Sure, what does he want?' Plugged in. Formulaic. Productive. The Cult in action.

'Oh, just a favor he needs that only I can do. If he wasn't such a good friend I might not do it. That reminds me, Don's sending his private jet for me next week. If you sames aren't busy, you're welcome to fly with me to Lost Aimless. My good friend...'

The Fireman is peerless. Relentless. An omnipotent formula applied without discretion.

As he continues his application, Flow breaks into one of his comedy routines

'This ever happen to you? You drop an E, look in the mirror and see some prick with a finger up his ass? Then you realize, it's you! Haaa hahaa...'

I can't lie, that one gets me every time.

'Cracula, what's happenin bro?'

Same as five minutes ago Flow—Culting, formulizing, fitting in.

'You know what your problem is?'

Oh lord.

One of the Brazilo sames attempts English, 'Crackey, what we dooey aftee dinnee?' I feel like a ten-year-old whore in Phnom Penh, 'We goey niteey clubeey?' Is it over yet?

Despite my efforts, I can still hear *South of Fraunce* in the distance. Sitting opposite Dickless, Slave stares at me and eats a banana. Treimee is soooo drunk. The Reverend—evolved businessman—pitches God to inventors. Nowe speaks to me about DJs. The mother-to-be chugs vodka, stares suggestively at sames, and pops a Valium.

South of Fraunce. South of Fraunce. South of Fraunce.

My new and unnatural body chemistry taking its toll, I need a smoke.

Judas Bar—being massive, well funded, and built post-smoking ban—has a sort of indoor but outdoor stoge quarters. An all-glass rectangle situated in plain sight for all to see—aquarium, zoo, archaeological exhibit—living, breathing, smoking relics. Example of what not to do in the whitewashed Island. We make our way, Fireman and I, greeting good friends, inventors—staring at other men's sames. I ask Fireman for a light.

'Cracula, you know I'm really proud of you.'

Sensing a heart-to-heart brewing, I channel The Cult and plug in.

'I don't know how you can do it…around all these idiots and not get buzzed. It's really just medicinal, to put up with the damn sames. You think I can talk to them without a bottle of vodka? No way.'

Thinking, no, applying like a Cult member, I peer into The Fireman's soul. The man is well intended, big of heart. He's me, Noddy, Aeronymous, The Reverend, Lousifer.

'Hey, one of the Brazilian sames is into sames. I think we should put her and Slutskia together, see what happens. Did I tell you about the new one I met in Miami? Hold on that's my good friend Spree.' Can't fucking help himself.

Twenty-Eight

The next several days are a wave of repetition. Slutskia would start in on her responsibilities—parents, seester. I, newly noble, would speak of our responsibility. Present my formula for Cult living.

'Baybee, is not possible.'

I hear nothing, forge ahead. Construct entire civilizations in my brain. New religions. Religions without history. My daughter will be the priest, choir, congregation. A nonbeliever. The breadth of Angkor Wat, the calm of the Mediterranean. She will never orbit, a galaxy of supernovas. Have no need for moons.

'Baybee, we no haveeng money. I alcoholic. And what is dees Cult baybee? Is stupid.'

She will be immune to inventors, hip to ladder dwellers. Allergic to businessmen, my daughter. A native with an immigrant's heart. She shall transcend the need to transcend. My daughter shall be her own birthright.

When not fantasizing through arguments, I'm meeting with other Cult members. Cult meetings. Never was I more plugged in, part of a formula. We sit in circles and chant, whine. Oh, do these Cult bastards whine.

I just feel like I'm on the verge of leaving The Cult…
When I walk past a bar, all I think about is my past life, how I
loved it…
My cat died, I'm having a really tough time right now…

It's enough to drive you to the bottle!

Twenty-Nine

On the seventh day of the wave's repetition I kiss Slutskia goodbye as she leaves for work. Then, my buzzer rings.

'Who is it?'

'Lousifer. I need to talk to you.'

I buzz in my most regrettable transgression.

'Lous, what's up bro?' I know.

'I need to ask you something, and I want you to tell me the truth.'

The question already asked, I straighten my glasses and light a red.

'Did you sleep with Dulce after her and I got together?'

I toke my red, give Lousifer one. Inhale, exhale.

Straighten my glasses.

Look at Lousifer, the floor. Inhale. Exhale.

Our blues meet. I blink. Match souls with the only honest bastard I know. *The man saved my life…fucking gave me his oxygen.*

'No.'

I lied.

I make no attempt to rationalize my lie. The fact I was on crack. Her persistence. Her black eye. No, I'm a piece of shit. An oven-fresh pile of elephant dung.

'Are you sure? Not one night fucked up?'

Dulce, what a hustler. Conjuror of emotions. A damn sorceress. Of course I know of multiple other guys she's fucked since being with Lous. Straight men, gay men, battalions. Entire cities, fashion weeks, music conferences. It matters not.

'No.'

'OK, I believe you. Wanna go for a jog?'

Sure, I'll go for a jog.

He heads back to Tenth and B to change. I replace my glasses with contacts. I do this with the lights off, afraid of my reflection.

We trot to the Dead Side Highway.

Running south towards Jellis Island, The Statue of Liberty, no words are spoken. Volumes. Annotated. Translated.

Taking in The Hudson, I know I belong at the bottom. Below the rats, snakes, snitches. I lied to the only honest bastard I know. He should have let me die. I'll fasten rocks to my head, jump in. No boulders, drown in the scum. *Why had I lied?* I could reach out to The Fireman, ask his advice. What worked for him in the past? What formula? Was this The Cult's doing? This lying? Had I again channeled Mill? Lying as altruism.

We run on.

Past the battery. Past mommies with strollers, past the fishing rods and into the tourists waiting for the Jellis Island Ferry.

We pause to catch our breath, Lousifer and Lie.

'Son, I don't know why the fuck she would say that.'

Me neither. Lousifer appears to have caught his breath, I'm still gasping.

Heading back up the Dead Side, we pick up the pace. I hang my head and visualize Chinese water torture, the guillotine, spontaneous human combustion. Ahh…but I'm a father to be. Must carry on

We bust a right on Canal, up Greenwich, right on Spring and stop at 109. Opposite Evolution.

'Alright son, I'll hit you up later.'

I slither up the stairs.

Thirty

Self-loathing and looking ahead eat up the next few hours. I try numbing myself via dotcomming—google, google, google, liespace, asmallturd, blewtube, racebook. I order sindemand and Demarco's, call Cult members. Still certain I deserve The Hudson bottom, I hear the door.

'Slutskia, what's up my dear?'

Every same same in the world is hatched with the ability to sense weakness, injury, smell blood. Slutskia's seed carrying only enhances this birthright. She can taste my loathing, hear my predicament.

'Baybee, I go back Russia hav abortion.'

Capitalizing on my state, she proclaims this with an unheard-of confidence and certainty. I won't allow myself to float away as usual. Can't. I must focus on the next few minutes. Critical. Life changing. Life ending.

'Babe, we talked about this already. We're having this kid.'

'Baybee I no give fauk, is up me. I spoke my mom already, she say I have abortion tuu. I buy ticket tuuday, I going.'

'Slutskia, fuck your mom! She's a greedy bitch. Does she ever call to ask for anything except money? Fuck her, she's just worried you won't be working for a few months. Let her fucking starve.'

'Baybee, fauk u! Is my mom, no u.'

'And what does your Dad have to say?'

'He say nauthing.'

'Well, he fucking should. Call your fucking mother right now, let me talk to that bitch.'

'Baybee, she no speaking eenglish. Anyway baybee, I go in three day.'

Mission critical. I move in close. Eyes to eyes, a blue swamp.

'Slutskia, listen to me very fucking carefully. You are not having any goddamn abortion. You are not going to fucking Moscow. Look at me! You fucking hear me!'

'Yes baybee, I duu!'

'You selfish bitch! So help me God, if you have an abortion I'll kill you myself!'

'Fauk u bastaard!'

I make for the door. *Who can I call?* Aeronymous? He is a Cult member, and despite himself, a friend. A decent soul.

'Yo, what up son?'

'Meet me in front of Balthazar, I need to talk.'

'See you there.'

I fly down my steps and turn left. Past Broadway, over Crosby, to the bench in front of Balthazar. Order a black coffee and light a red. Sitting. Waiting. I watch all the dogs walk by, all the strollers.

'Cracula, what's the deal?'

'Aeronymous, sit down man. Listen, I need to talk to somebody about some things. But please keep this between us, yeah?'

'No doubt son.'

I know he won't. Can't. No matter.

'So here's the deal...I haven't told anyone else this, no one. Slutskia's pregnant.'

'Yeah?'

'Yeah, and right now shit's hittin the fan.'

'What's up?'

'Well, I wanna have the kid. Straight up. She's been saying from the jump that she wants an abortion. You know her situation with her parents back in Russia.'

'Word. But how are you gonna take care of...'

'Aeronymous! That's not why I'm fucking talking to you.'

'Sorry.'

'Anyway, I was sure she'd come around. You know, me being in The Cult and all, but today she fucking comes home and tells me she bought a ticket for Moscow, that she's talked to her cunt of a mom, and she's having an abortion.'

'Word?'

'Yeah. Then I lost it. Told her I'd kill her, grabbed her fucking arm, all that.'

'So you really want this kid?'

'Yeah man. There's no reason not to, and I know it's a girl.'

'Yeah?'

'Yeah. Will you take a walk with me back there, try and talk to her?'

'No doubt.'

Not sure if it's my newfound cult disposition or something greater, but making our way over Spring I sense the need to pick up the pace. *Urgency.* Crossing Mercer I'm in a sprint.

Key inserted, I take the stairs two by two. Galloping. Fling my door open.

Thirty-One

Floating on the kitchen table is a single-minded sheet of paper—
a note. Four words. It reads:

I GO RUSSIA, BY

estaba soñando

there is a tiny five-foot ledge between our loft and the
neighbor's. its only purpose to house a ladder used for changing
light bulbs atop the living room. slutskia, the mother of my
daughter, has disrobed, tied my crackberry cord around her neck,
climbed the ladder, fastened the other end to the top step and let
go her feet

for three seconds (hours?) i'm frozen. immobile. petrified.

I re-attach to the living, run over to her blue and purple body, rip
the cord off and lay her face up.

a tub of ice

I slap her face. Left hand. Right hand. Left. Right. Left.
Right. Left. Right. Left Right. Left. Right. Left. Right. Left.
Right. Left. Right. *Aeronymous, fucking call 911!*

I attempt mouth to mouth. Breathing. Chest pounding.
Shaking. Screaming. *Pulse?* Temple. Neck. Stomach.

womb

My blues meet Aeronymous. Nothing. Drained of thought.
Outside wit. Non-formulaic.

collapse

I attempt tears, but find the road blocked. I reach for
convulsions, too far. Anger meets me halfway. Rage.
surrender

I wish to trade my soul for Slutskia's, resuscitate her. Watch
over her like a dark angel until she births my daughter, then slice

her head off. cook it up, slam it   The cowardice witch. *Not even a note!* Did she not owe our daughter a goddamn note? A letter? did she not owe her an epic

Fuck her. Fuck The Cult. Fuck God.

Thirty-Two

Embalmed when the police come, the paramedics. Aeronymous does the talking.

I remain motionless as they carry away the bag. The bodies.

'Sir, is there anyone that should be called?'

'Sir?'

I got someone to call.

estaba soñando

I was an onion, in human form.
Sweating. Itching.
itching, sweating.
I was open, porous.

Onion tears ran down my onion cheeks onto my onion tongue.
I scratched onion balls with onion nails.

I pulled my onion hair until it fell in my onion mouth,
tasted like onions.
Raw onions.

I scratched so hard a layer of the onion shed.
Feeling in tune, I kept scratching.

another layer.
another

My onion hands were covered in onion blood,
I scratched on.

I scratched my onion nose until it fell to my onion feet.
I scratched my onion face until I removed my onion skull.

I scratched my onion eyes until they cried no more onion tears.
I scratched on.

I scratched until there was no more onion blood, onion skin.
No more onion.

I was a fetus, human again.
No more than a heartbeat.
I was possibility.
I was possible.

I came to, I wasn't dreaming.
I was at Noddy's place, arm bleeding.
I need another hit.

'Noddy...Noddy.'

yeah?

'Load me up another one. Same white, little more D.'

I was aboard the spaceship Assimilator, bound for Gleisica. The first human to enter the constellation Libra. Our first stop was the capital, Perg. I'm to meet the Queen, discuss intergalactic diplomacy.

We dined in the Perg Palace, joined by Gleisican dignitaries and politicians. Drank 1000-year-old ring wine, ate natives and raw Gleisican vegetables. The Queen told me of their utopian state, their evolution into compartmentalization. The dichotomy of Gleisican civilization, what the Queen referred to as harmony. I was to tour Perg and two other cities the following day, her daughter my guide.

I woke the following morning to coffee from the Sagittarian minefields, scrowalactyl (an indigenous flying creature) eggs, and fruit from their closest moon, Darby A. I was bathed by fluorescent eunuchs and outfitted in the latest Perg wears.

As it so happens Gleisica has a weekly solar eclipse every Darkday, today. Darkdays are dedicated to Pergan nighttime activities. We began our tour in quadrant LE.

It should be mentioned that Gleisicans come in many colors: purple, green, rust, blue, orange, sienna, turquoise, olive, lavender, cyan, firebrick…and appear to be equally displaced throughout Perg.

Makiva, the Princess, has the dark brown skin of her mother, save for her British racing green head. (Rumor has it, her nipples turn blue on contact?)

We started our day of night by taking the Assimilator ground hover craft (Aghc) to quadrant LE. The place seemed interesting enough, lots of Perg bands and what not. All the fellas in tight white pants, outlining their evolved Gleisican cocks. The alien sames all topless in plaid skirts, intergalactic combat boots, red hair. The eunuchs rocked indigo jumpsuits, checkered hats, ivory slippers.

Our first stop was Milky Way, the new LE hot spot. It was retro night every Darkday. 'Earth Darkdays' they called it. The place has a ten-mile antennae on the roof, literally catching and broadcasting our planet's transmissions as they rolled in from the cosmos. Apparently the 80s were just arriving. Mötley Crüe, Def Leppard, Van Halen, Poison, and GNR blasted throughout Milky Way. The DJ keeping an alien ear to Amoeban and English FM transmissions.

Drinking and smoking were banned in Perg, but every 30 minutes Milky Way released a duster.

A duster is like bombing a house for cockroaches, a miniature mushroom cloud. Makiva told me it contained WHB, HST, PKD, and Amoeban-style LSD. 'Don't tell the Queen I didn't take my filtration pill before we came.' don't worry honey

Post-duster, the DJ picked up KROQ and blasted Cinderella. *Could I not have visited a few years later?* Oh well, I'm loaded.

Dusted, Makiva began to loosen up. actually looked hot, green head and all. She told me how lovely it was to meet an Earthling, tells me she loves our music. How's the Cold War show going? *Dallas*?

I asked her why no one here notices me, being an Earthling. and her? The Princess. 'Oh they do, the LE Pergs are just too cool to give us the satisfaction. As soon as we leave they'll make fun of us, talk about your shoes.' *My Chucks?*

We took in another duster and boarded the Aghc. Our next stop quadrant W.

The Pergs in Quadrant W did not hide their shock at seeing an Earthling, or The Princess. We were ushered into the newest W outpost, Sol. We signed autographs, posed for pictures, and were slipped contraband. Makiva explained the red pills were whiskey time-release capsules, the white pills serotonin boosters (with a one-hour cutoff), the blue pills instant comedown. *I must be dreaming.* Still dusted, I popped a red and a white, felt at home.

All Perg society lined up to greet Makiva, pay homage, alien name-drop.

Makiva, I went to boarding school with your father on Gleisoma...
I just love your dress, really brings out your head...
Are you summering in the rings again? We should share a ship...
Feel free to use my moon house any time...

Jesus, what sycophants. She seemed to take it all in stride, told me it comes with the territory.

Popping another red, we board the Aghc and head across
Gleisica to the city of A.

Makiva explained that A is Gleisica's university town. Five
years required of all Gleisicans after their tenth birthday.

'Ten seems a bit young?'

'Well Cracula, we Gleisicans only sleep once a year, for three
days.'

yeah?

'Has something to do with us having more liquid water than
Earth, 35 moons, and a red dwarf for a star. By ten, Gleisicans
have seen our entire planet. Most have even been to a few
moons.'

We park the Aghc in the town center, across from the university
library. Makiva informs me that it is finals week for the seniors.

The library is overflowing with students, holograms, 14-year-
olds. Only they are separated by color. blue with blue, grey with
grey, purple, magenta, lavender, khaki.

'What's up with the color segregation?'

'We've never been able to figure it out. Before and after
university, Gleisicans of all colors mix. Play together, work
together, procreate. For some reason they take it upon
themselves to congregate by color at university.'

yeah?

'Each color group reverts to the tradition of their ancestors.
They speak in ancient dialects, celebrate forgotten holidays,

bring up past atrocities. Of course with eons of multi-color-limbed Gleisicans, it makes it difficult for some students. Can you believe they actually have to choose? It's tough, I know. Deciding between head and body, arm and leg. But they're just kids, they get over it.'

I thought that pretty fucking odd and popped another two reds. Makiva popped a white, made me swear not to tell her mom.

We made our way back to The Assimilator.

'Where to?'

'Our last stop Cracula. Tourie.'

It turned out Tourie was Gleisica's most distant moon. Damn near its rings. The trip was turbulent, in and out of competing gravity fields and whatnot.

Tourie in sight, a change came over Makiva, her disposition. Her green face suddenly glowed with royal spoils. She gazed right though me in anticipation. resolute and determined.

As the landing gear released, Makiva handed me a black pill.

'Cracula, take this.'

Feeling on foreign land for the first time, I obliged. We walked down The Assimilator ramp, onto the moon.

Tourie was a desert of green sand. bleak The red dwarf out of sight.

'So what's the black pill for? You trying to take advantage of me?' The Princess was not amused.

'Cracula, the black pill is to keep you alive. Forced life. No matter the pain and suffering you are to endure...HA HA HA...'

Makiva's eyes bled red, her tone final.

'You are to spend eternity on Tourie. You will never die.' She boarded The Assimilator.

I was frozen, embalmed. My blood icicles, organs stone, eyes glass. Every pore stabbed with infected needles.

Conjuring all my strength I lifted my tundra'd right foot, took a step.

Flames shot up my right calf, knee, thigh. Fireballs slammed through my eyes. Acid flowed through my veins. I shit magma and melted in two seconds. only to be restored in one. Searing flesh my milieu. My tongue roasted before I could scream. again and again

I managed another step.

Permafrost. The needles returned. Sharper. Icicles broke, stones cracked, glass shattered. *rebuilt* Frozen beyond noise.

another step

Incineration. Epidermis bubbled, blues roasted, atria exploded. Bones ashed. and again

Step

Fire. Ice.

At the stake. Extinct.

cracula

'cracula…Cracula…'

Fuck me, I'm at The Sheik's.

'You OK?'

'What the hell happened last night?'

'You showed up around two, threatened to kill my doorman, dripped blood all over my place, shot something in your arm, and passed out.'

'Sorry Sheik.'

'No worries. You wanna hit this?'

'I'm good. What're you working on?'

'Cover for *Newsweak*. They're officially endorsing Obama for president.'

Yeah?

'They want me to morph the faces of Bill, Hillary, Martha Jefferson, Nelson Mandela, Charlton Heston, OJ, Britney, and Oprah. But still make it look like a "shiny and vibrant presidential Barack." '

You're kidding?

'I wish.'

The Sheik rolls a joint. I call the deli and the dealer.

Thirty-Three

I come to at 109 Spring. The scene of the crime. The Reverend asks me how I'm doing. Do I need anything?

Sure, pour us two glasses of whiskey. He obliges and I light a red.

'You know Cracula, this may not be the time to discuss it...'

Is there ever?

'...but there probably never will be. I'm really sorry about Slutskia. And Aeronymous told me about the pregnancy.'

Of course he did.

'I want you to know that your child, and it was a child...'

I feel this is where we begin to part.

'...your child's in heaven, and that God loves him, or her.'

Her.

'I know it's hard to understand, but He is all-loving, all-knowing.'

Does The Reverend not understand I bleed as Shaula gives light? After all the years can he not surmise I'm unable to open neatly wrapped packages? Never made it past the bow. He continues his delivery, my Reverend. A UPS driver.

'You need to pray for your child's soul. Pray for the soul of Slutskia.'

I light another red and lock my jaw. Pray my love for The Reverend will halt the outburst brewing in my gut.

'Cracula, I pray to God for all three of you.'

Too late.

'Reverend, if there is this cowering pissant of a god, let this punk come down and have a good goddamn chat with me. Let him explain this love you talk about . Let him explain this taking of souls. Let him explain your blind trance. If this burrowing crab showed himself I'd rip out his heart, I know he doesn't have any fucking balls! And while I'm at it, FUCK YOU and your solace-seeking atonal-toned, voluntarily blindfolded Jesus-imitating path. Fuck all you motherfuckers, get the hell out of my place!'

Content I've placed myself outside his prayer sphere, I light another red and call my dealer.

Thirty-Four

Reverend out of the way, my path is set. Everyone else an avoidable text message.

Aeronymous
Yo son, The Cult can still work for you. Call me.

Tambourine
Hey C, let me no if u nead 2 talk
I'm with u in thpirit
Xo
Tambourine(thpirit)
Ps let me kno if you want 2 c my thpiritual advisr

Lousifer
U good?

Flow
Yo bro, fuck it. You win some, lose some. Lets hang later

Slave
Let me know if you need your cock sucked

Fireman
Hey Cracula, I know what you're going thru. I got two new same-sames for tonight.
It will take your mind off all this. Trust me.

Hugatcha
Have you read that Genet?

Feather

Noddy
Fuck these idiots let's get loaded

word

Thirty-Five

The next weeks (months?) are spent in a steady state of
detachment. I shuttle between 109 Spring and The Noddy Inn.
Doorbells are ignored and carefully answered. Texts repeated,
phone shut off, sindemand gone black with the dotcom. Books
avoided.

I breathe and dream delivery. No longer in fear of helicopters,
federal agents, aliens. I welcome them. We converse at length,
coexist.

It appears they speak amongst themselves as well. Have an
arrangement of sorts. Partners in a timeshare.

The Black Hawks stick to the mornings, 9:00–11:00. They
usually land in the kitchen, squeezing in through my window.
(On occasion the pilot flies right up the damn stairs, *what must
the neighbors think?*) When they ask, I bring the guys whiskey,
a smoke,

a line.

But mostly we stay out of each other's way.   talk at a distance
They always manage to leave when I'm not looking.

The FBI cats are a bit more high-maintenance. The whiskey has
to be Johnnie Walker, beer Heineken. The coffee strong. They
aren't big on the yack, look down on it to be honest. They arrive
3:00–9:00 in the PM, always incognito. They communicate with
each other on radio, jam my iPod.

Recently, they've hatched a plot to assassinate me. Take me out.
Eradicate, expunge. They've grown paranoid of my powers, my

knowledge. I know when they're coming though. Hell, I buzz them in.

Before they reach the door I'm in the sauna, temperature maxed. This cancels out the tracking chip they planted in my brain.

Midnight to five (always my favorite hours) are for the aliens. A supreme honor. Extraterrestrials, higher life forms, ILLEGALS. I'm the only human they've made contact with, confided their secrets.

They've been around for years, centuries really. Observing. Cultivating. Introducing mind control, the Tooth Fairy, Easter Bunny, Christianity. Electing presidents here and there.

We get on famously, the little blue guys and I. Not into whiskey, they bring their own alien absinthe, moon dust. Do the occasional blast with me. *Lo que sea.* I divulge my earthly tales—cavorting, indulging, exploring, proliferating, pendulating, evolving and revolving, matriculating, isolating, escaping, nodding, slamming.

The blue fellas wax speed of light, black holes, intergalactic sames, stellular dope. The sky life. They reveal the forces behind the universe—PROSTITUTION and NEPOTISM.

I produce pictures to match my adventures. They mainline my brain with a millennium of images. What a trip.

The 109 timeshare carries on for awhile. Tragically, the Feds begin stretching their daily intrusion, pushing the soldiers and aliens out. Eminent domain they call it.

I eventually tire of government intrusion, music blaring with the stereo off, prying neighbors. In need of a parachute, the doctor is called.

I exchange cash for medicine and sit on my couch.

Perusing the familiar warning label, I think it might apply. But hey, you're not supposed to drink on antibiotics either.

Covering my freckle, I indulge.

free fall

emergency chute

I was just below the clouds.
alive

I spread my wings and floated through the cumulus—not
wanting to see below.

Putting off my inevitable I shot up, out of the atmosphere.

I passed the moon, circled Mars, jetted past Jupiter, Saturn.
Touched down for a bottle of wine on Uranus.

A bump on Neptune.

Feeling just right, I headed for our star's last satellite.

Hovering above Tambourine, I flapped my wings. Too icy for
contact. I nodded a formulaic nod to her moons, they looked
crestfallen. *Was she content living so far from a star?* Cold and
lifeless? Did she mind the permafrost, the long revolution?
Tambourine told me she could always take solace in her moons,
they were consistent.

I wished her well and flew back towards the earth. Made another
stop on Uranus, took in the view.

Absolving my wings, I circled the rings, catapulted back through
the earth's atmosphere

I was greeted by a dark angel, Fred. He wanted to see my
credentials. *Why was I here?* He explained to me that The
Fireman now ruled the land and must approve all comers. *good*

friends only. I explained that we went way back, I wouldn't be long.

Checking my wings for contraband and running my ID, I revealed my fangs and was allowed safe passage.

Diving through the clouds I came across a floating Feather. I didn't bother saying hello.

Swooping below the billows, I saw a million-times tentacled Fireman sitting atop a volcano made of logs. He said hello and continued to talk to himself, good friends. A million Razors. Oblivious.

Skimming the water I journeyed west, the wind to my back.

Transcending the earth's oceans I came across a courtroom of sorts—supreme court on the sea. The Reverend was wearing a judge's robe and banging an imaginary gavel. In front of him were dolphins, sharks, sponges, starfish, crabs, sand. Each pleading their case. Why were *they* to be banished to land? Why not sea lions, eels, saltwater crocs? Having none of it, The Reverend banged his gavel.

I soared on.

I came upon an Everest-sized wave moving at blinding speed. Atop the wave surfed a chiseled Ken doll Aeronymous. He sipped beer and chatted with Neil Young. Satisfied.

Sailing on, I came across an odd Slave Carsons. He appeared to be sex-changed, with long blonde hair and a Cracula tattoo above his ass. His feet were over his shoulder as he thrust something in his contrived vagina.

I soared on.

I came across a ragged beach, an historic beach, a battlefield. I
hovered and observed. Below me lay the world's great
warriors—Alexander, Genghis Kahn, Sitting Bull, Custer...Up
ahead was a Samurai in red armor. I butterflied over to the
victor.

Lousifer? He dismounted his horse and sewed Dulce back
together. They seamed at ease with the world. I loved them both.

I soared on.

I circled the globe, not knowing my destination.

Noticed an abandoned Amoeba.

I touched down on the beach where 109 used to be and spotted a
serpent-tailed Slutskia surrounded by goddesses. John Wayne.
A mermaid served my blood.

I set sail one last time.

Closing my eyes, I left my fate to the wind.

She tossed me in the ocean, cast me on a beach.

My wings lost. Detained and isolated. I felt at home.
Indigenous.

The sun was soon to set behind the ocean, a full moon rising.

I drank my wine and opened my eyes. Emerging from the ocean
in front of me was a little girl, blue-eyed. White wings. She
walked over to me and met my blues.

Relieved, I accepted the inevitable.

The verdict rendered, loudest echo I've ever heard.

Thanks Mark, Nicky, Terban.

Special thanks to Sara Rosen for reeling me in.

Thanks to Daniel Power, Craig Cohen, Robert Avellan, Wes Del Val, and everyone else at powerHouse Books.

Brantly Martin has been working in New York City nightlife
for the past eight years, hosting weekly parties at various
downtown Manhattan venues. He was born in Houston
and now lives in Rome.